TO LOVE AGAIN

It is December, 1813. Two small girls are bored, lonely, and travelling to their grandmother's house for Christmas. Their father is a widower, barely able to walk after fighting Napoleon, their nursemaid is not very bright, and their governess has no enthusiasm or imagination. Then, at a coaching inn, some of their horses are stolen. Their only comfort is from a widowed lady who is also stuck there . . .

PHILIPPA CAREY

TO LOVE AGAIN

Waterford City & County Libraries

WITHDRAWN

Complete and Unabridged

LINFORD
Leicester

First published in Great Britain in 2018

First Linford Edition
published 2021

A catalogue record for this book is available
from the British Library.

ISBN 978–1–4448–4727–7

Published by
Ulverscroft Limited
Anstey, Leicestershire

Printed and bound in Great Britain by
TJ Books Ltd., Padstow, Cornwall

This book is printed on acid-free paper

Come in to My Parlour

James, Earl Benfield, walked slowly and painfully down the road, leaning heavily on his two walking sticks. There was a cold wind whistling through the bare branches of the roadside trees.

He shivered, despite having his coat collar turned up high and his beaver hat pulled down as far as it would go. He had been desperate for some quiet and some fresh air, after sharing a crowded carriage all day with his two young daughters, their nurse and their governess.

It had been tempting to travel in the second carriage with his valet and their mountain of baggage, but he didn't feel he could. He always felt guilty about how little time he spent with his daughters after their mother had died, but still, it had been an exhausting day.

Both girls had soon got bored, fidgety and tired of watching the scenery go by. Their governess had tried to keep them occupied, but they were not in the mood,

1

so she quickly got frustrated, too, and irritable in her attempts.

Perhaps he should have put the girl's nursemaid in the other carriage to make a little more space. She was good-natured and hard-working, but a bit empty-headed and unable to entertain the girls, either.

He had originally intended to travel a little further today as well, but enough was enough. They had all finished the day tired, bad-tempered and grumpy.

If only he had been able to ride beside the carriage, he thought, but it was equally impossible. The girls needed his company and in any case, he couldn't ride a horse all day now. Curse the French, curse Napoleon and curse the army surgeon who had set his broken bones so poorly.

He noticed a carriage coming down the road and wasted no time in moving slowly to the side. Moving out of the way quickly was no longer an option. He watched the carriage as it passed and caught a brief glimpse of a lady who glanced at him as she went by.

James turned to watch the carriage as it entered the inn yard. He should go back to the inn. It had been a short walk, and welcome, but his legs were already too painful to go further. Besides, now he was in the open air, the chill of the November wind was very noticeable and he was happy to turn his back to it. The fresh air was just a bit too fresh.

His daughters would be eating their tea in the private parlour and while they did, he could rest his legs and try some of the local brew in the undoubtedly warm public bar.

★ ★ ★

Emma was glad to reach the inn. She was tired of sitting in a carriage all day. Her maid Molly had a lot of common sense and was very competent, but not what Emma would consider scintillating company. Emma was always revived by a good strong cup of tea and now she was more than ready for one and a piece of cake to go with it. As she entered the inn, the landlord bustled forward, wiping his hands on his apron.

'Good evening. Lady Collins, I presume?' he said.

'Yes. You have a reserved room and private parlour for me, I believe?'

He grimaced and sucked air through his teeth.

'I have the room, but I am afraid the parlour is at present occupied. A titled gentleman arrived and he insisted very strongly upon taking the parlour for his daughters, the nursemaid and their governess.

'They are all taking afternoon tea at the moment, but will surely be finished soon. I shall get the maid to take you up some hot water so that you can refresh yourself in the meantime.'

'There seems little point in sending ahead a reservation if you then give the room away,' Emma said peevishly. For the last ten miles, she had had her heart set upon the tea and cake before doing anything else.

'I do beg your pardon, madam, the

4

fault is entirely mine,' a deep masculine voice behind her said.

She whirled to see who else might be ready to annoy her. It was the man in the road she had glimpsed from her carriage.

Surprise caught her tongue. He was not a decrepit old man on walking sticks as she had at first thought, but a decrepit young man on walking sticks.

His face was slightly shadowed by the upright collar of his coat, but his features were arresting. Except for the tired and dejected expression on his face and a slight stoop, he was definitely rather handsome and probably in his early thirties or late twenties, most likely little older than she was.

Even resting on his walking sticks, he was still a shade taller than Emma. A strand of brown hair poked out from under his hat and across his forehead.

As the lady had turned to face him, James could see past the brim of her bonnet. She was a young and unhappy vision of loveliness. She had a heart-shaped face, marred only by an angry frown and pursed rosy lips. She had a trim but shapely figure and was well dressed in a dark green gown, with a fur-lined cloak which had been opened at the front.

An aristocratic voice had only emphasised that this was a lady of quality who expected to be made comfortable.

After a tiring and stressful day, he did not need more aggravation from this assertive lady.

'I must apologise. My daughters were fractious after a day cooped up in a carriage and I didn't know what else to do with them.

'I am afraid I browbeat the landlord here into letting us have the room for a while. If you give me a few minutes I shall eject them so that you may have your parlour.' He turned to the stairs, put both walking sticks in one hand and reached for the banister with the other.

'Oh, wait,' Emma said, feeling contrite. There was no need for her to inflict her discontent on other people when they had been perfectly sensible and reasonable, especially if they were merely trying

6

to care for their children.

'Perhaps we might share, if the room is not too small?' She looked at the land-lord, who nodded gratefully.

'Thank you,' James said. He paused, then held out a hand, as it was obviously difficult for him to bow. 'Benfield, at your service, ma'am.'

She shook his hand.

'Lady Collins. I am so sorry to incon-venience you, but I too am weary from sitting in a carriage all day and desperate for some tea.'

'Not at all, it is we who have incon-venienced you. If you would follow me I will ensure that they make space for you and then leave you in peace to drink your tea.'

He started up the stairs, step by slow step. Emma resisted the temptation to help him. He would probably be offended, and besides, they had only just met.

Instead, she turned to the landlord and told him to send tea and cake up to the parlour, have someone show her maid to their room and to get someone to take her bags up.

By then, James had progressed sufficiently up the stairs so that Emma could
follow but would not seem to be crowd-
ing him impatiently.

Sad Revelations

As they entered the parlour, four sets of eyes looked up and then over James's shoulder to see Emma behind him.

'Girls, Miss Trellis, make your bow to Lady Collins, if you please,' James said. 'We have stolen her private parlour and she has graciously agreed to share it with us.'

The two young girls, nursemaid and their governess rose to their feet and curtseyed to Emma who nodded in return.

'Lady Collins, my daughters, Lady Sarah,' he said, indicating the elder, 'and Lady Helen, and their governess Miss Trellis — and their nursemaid Amy.' He pulled out a chair at the empty end of the table for Emma.

Emma sat and smiled at the girls, who smiled tremulously back, before clambering back up into their seats again.

'If you will excuse me,' James said, 'I shall go back downstairs and see that tea is sent up without delay.' He headed for the door.

He still needed some time to himself, aided by a pint of the landlord's best, to restore his good humour. Besides, he did not want to be obliged to make small talk with a stranger, even if she was a very attractive stranger.

Miss Trellis was perfectly capable of taking charge in the parlour and making sure Lady Collins was not troubled.

Emma looked at the girls who had glanced at each other, but had not spoken. They were obviously sisters and both had dark red hair, presumably like their mother, as they didn't resemble their father very much at all.

Their hair fell in ringlets down to their shoulders and they wore white dresses sprinkled with embroidery. Sarah's was fastened with a wide green satin sash and Helen's with a similar blue.

They were both pretty girls and very properly sitting up straight at the table. As they were both fairly small, Emma supposed they were sitting on cushions. They were quite young, perhaps eight and six years old, and seemed worn out.

Their governess, in a dark grey gown buttoned to the neck, looked severe and Emma suspected they had been told not to speak unless they were spoken to. This was easily solved.

'Your father said you were tired from spending all day travelling. Have you come far?'

'From Oakham, my lady,' Lady Sarah said.

'And it was very long and very tedious,' her younger sister Lady Helen grumbled.

Miss Trellis frowned at her but said nothing.

'Oh, I know what you mean,' Emma replied. 'I've come all the way from Spalding and there was hardly anything to see along the way. The countryside in that direction is quite flat and not at all exciting.'

'It's better in the summer when the trees are in leaf and there are flowers to see,' Sarah agreed, 'but at this time of year it all looks very bleak.'

'And when you have seen one sheep,

you have seen them all,' Helen said, with an accusing glance at Miss Trellis.

Just then, a maid entered the room with a tray full of tea things and a plate of small cakes. The girls addressed themselves to the food on their plates while Emma poured herself a cup of tea. After savouring her tea and sighing with relief, she glanced at the cakes.

'Do you recommend any of these?' she asked, waving a hand at the cakes and glancing up at the girls.

Both girls paused and peered over the table to see what Emma had on the cake dish.

'I liked the Banbury cakes best,' Sarah said in a considered fashion.

'I liked the jam tarts better,' Helen said.

'And I didn't like the Marchpane,' Sarah added.

'No, our cook makes it much nicer than they do here,' Helen said.

'In that case I shall avoid the Marchpane and try the Banbury cakes and jam tarts instead,' Emma said, putting one of each on her plate. 'Are you going far tomorrow?' she continued.

'We are going to Baldock to visit Grandmother,' Sarah said.

'It's her sixtieth birthday,' Helen added, 'and Father said the whole family is going, so we'll see our uncle, aunt and cousins. Father said we must be on our best behaviour and a credit to him.'

'Is your mother already there?'

'No, our mother died of a fever two years ago,' Helen said, looking mournful. 'I can hardly remember her.'

Sarah poked her sister in the ribs with her elbow and frowned at her.

'Oh, I see,' Emma said, realising her question had been tactless. She should probably have guessed as much if they were travelling with their father only. 'I'm so sorry to hear that, it's very sad.'

Miss Trellis looked embarrassed.

'Come along, girls, finish what you have on your plates before we go upstairs to bed.'

Sarah looked rebellious, as if she thought it was too early for bed.

'Lady Collins, are you going far?' she asked.

'I am going to London, to Stratton Street, to stay with my brother and his family until the New Year.'

'Father says we will going to London after Grandmother's birthday to see some of the sights, but I would rather be at home.

'The snow in London always seems grey and dirty and it's very cold to be driving around looking at old uninteresting buildings. It would be better to be at home and play in the nice clean snow around our house.'

Emma blinked. She was a little surprised at such plain speaking by a very young girl. She had the impression that this Lady Sarah was clever, and old for her years, being obviously thoughtful and well spoken.

'Old buildings? Are you not going to see the menagerie at the Tower of London or Astley's Amphitheatre for instance?'

'No, Father can't manage the walking and Miss Trellis is visiting her family for

Christmas.' Sarah looked resentfully at her governess.

'Oh. That is unfortunate,' Emma said, 'but couldn't your maid take you?' She looked at Amy who looked startled at the prospect.

'No, there's nobody,' a glum Sarah said, shaking her head. 'Amy would get lost.'

Amy nodded agreement to this blunt appraisal.

'That is quite enough now, Sarah, it is time both of you went to bed. We have another long day ahead of us tomorrow. Say goodnight to Lady Collins,' Miss Trellis said.

Both Sarah and Helen looked sad. Emma wasn't sure if it was the prospect of going to bed when they would prefer to talk or the prospect of a dreary time in London.

The four of them rose, said goodnight and filed out of the room, leaving Emma with her thoughts and the remaining cakes.

Emma's thoughts were sad, too. She

hadn't been married to Peter very long before he went off to war three years ago and never came back. If they had been married longer, she might have had a daughter or son to care for, to talk to, and to remind her of Peter as well.

How she wished she had two daughters just like Sarah and Helen. Her brother had three sons, but nephews simply weren't the same and she hardly ever saw them anyway.

A Calming Influence

Emma woke up to the noise of shouting men and horses whinnying, snorting and stamping their feet. She opened her eyes to realise it was still dark but there were flickering lights showing through the curtains.

Fire, she realised immediately, and clambered out of bed to see what was going on. As she went to the window and pulled the curtains back, her maid Molly joined her and they both looked out to see the stables at the back of the inn were on fire.

'Quickly, Molly, we must get dressed in case the fire spreads,' Emma urged.

'Yes, my lady, but I think we should be safe. Look, the wind is blowing the flames away from us and the stables have a tiled roof. It must be just the straw and wood inside that's burning.'

Emma hesitated as she surveyed the scene outside. Molly was no fool and almost certainly right. The stable yard was full of men rushing around and frightened horses looking for a way to escape the flames.

A group of men were pushing the carriages away from the burning building.

'You may be right, but we must get dressed anyway, in case the wind changes direction.'

Minutes later they went downstairs to the public bar with Molly clutching her mistress's jewel box to her chest. In the bar they found Lord Benfield with his family group.

'Ah, good, I was about to send Miss Trellis upstairs to find you,' he said. 'My valet and the grooms are helping outside, but obviously a cripple like me has to keep out of the way.'

Emma was surprised by the bitterness in his voice, but could see his point. Presumably he was frustrated he couldn't help in the emergency like the other men and humiliated that he had to stay with the women.

'I suggest we stay here for the time being. We are right by the front door should we need to leave in a hurry, but there is no point in standing in the cold and catching a chill,' he continued.

'Lady Collins, we're scared,' Sarah said in a voice that trembled. 'If the fire comes this way, we'll have to go outside, where all the horses will be frightened and rushing about.'

'Father says we have to keep away from nervous horses,' Helen added, 'otherwise one might fall on us and break our legs as happened to him.'

Emma looked in surprise at them telling her these things, as she was essentially a stranger. She could see the girls really were afraid and shaking, despite the presence of their father, nurse and governess. Her heart went out to them, so she joined them on the settle and put an arm around each of them.

'Now there's no need to be afraid,' she said, 'my maid Molly is clever and says the wind is blowing the fire away from us.'

Everybody glanced at Molly, who looked self-conscious, but nodded vigorously anyway.

'Even if the fire did come this way, we could simply go out of the front door over there and there aren't any horses at the front. All the horses are in the yard at the back, so we will be quite safe.'

Emma hoped this was the case, because she suspected that horses were leaving the yard at the back to get away from the fire and it was unlikely anybody would try to stop them, whichever way the horses went. They could be anywhere.

However, this was a detail that two small girls didn't need to consider. Both looked somewhat reassured, so she cuddled them closer.

She looked up to see their father looking blankly at the tableau they presented. He closed his mouth which had been hanging open. She frowned slightly at him, daring him to object, but he merely gave a slight nod as if he had understood the message.

'Yes, quite so,' was all he said to confirm the opinion, before pulling out a chair to sit down.

Emma wondered how to divert the

girls from worrying about the situation.

'Well,' she said to them, 'why don't I tell you a story while we wait?'

'A story?' Sarah asked. 'What kind of story?'

Emma looked down at Sarah, wondering what would be most distracting or appropriate. She noticed again, the dark red hair of Sarah and her sister. Red hair was unfashionable, not that it mattered much to small girls.

However, it might not stop some people making disparaging remarks, so there was merit in making it into something positive. Thus, not Goldilocks, who was a selfish girl and then ran off when confronted. Instead a confident Rubylocks, who would stand her ground with the three bears. But bears were brown, so not bears, either, but . . . foxes.

'Let me see,' Emma said, putting a theatrical finger to her bottom lip. 'How about the story of Rubylocks and the three foxes?'

'Don't you mean Goldilocks and the three bears?' Helen asked.

'Oh, no, Goldilocks was a quite different girl. Rubylocks was a much nicer girl who had lovely red hair just like yours.'

Emma proceeded to tell them the story which was vaguely similar to the one about the three bears.

Rubylocks was someone who politely asked the foxes for help when she got lost in their woods. The foxes gave her food and let her rest before guiding her home, so it was much more positive story. She quickly had everybody's rapt attention, even their father, especially when she made noises like the foxes barking.

As she finished the tale, the back door opened and a man with a sooty face entered.

'It's all under control now, my lord. A lamp had fallen on to some straw. The grooms are making sure all the embers are damped and the horses are safely out in the meadow. You may go back to bed now if you wish, but we will all have a late start in the morning. It's too dark until then to clear out all the ash and retrieve the horses.'

'Thank you, Norton,' James said to his valet. 'When you've finished helping them outside, just clean yourself up and go to back to bed. Don't worry about me, I can get myself upstairs and to bed.'

'Lady Collins, may we have another story, please?' Sarah asked with a pleading face.

'No, no, Sarah,' her father said, 'you must let Lady Collins go back to bed now, as the rest of us should as well. Say your thanks, and back upstairs the pair of you.'

Sarah pouted a little and sagged with disappointment.

'Thank you, Lady Collins, that was a wonderful story. I do wish we had time for another.'

'I'm afraid not. It's time we all went back to sleep after all this excitement. We will all have another long day tomorrow,' Emma said. 'Perhaps your father, or Miss Trellis, or Amy could tell you one on your journey tomorrow.'

Sarah glanced at her father, then her governess and then Amy with a look of resignation before taking her sister's hand.

'Good night, Lady Collins,' both girls said before they went off upstairs with the servants.

James waited until they had all gone before turning to Emma.

'I am much obliged to you, Lady Collins, for so effectively taking their minds off the fire and calming them. It is at times like this that we all regret the loss of their mother two years ago. A father, governess and nurse are no real substitute.

'Good night and thank you. I hope we will see you before we depart tomorrow.' He stood and made his way slowly upstairs.

Emma watched him go. Poor girls. It was clear why they had befriended Emma so readily. Their governess seemed to be dry, humourless, without imagination and not the sort to mother two lonely little girls.

The nurse didn't appear to be very bright and their father had his own problems. Thank goodness the girls had each other.

Emma rose to her feet to return to her bed, wondering what the stables would look like in the daytime and how long it would take to retrieve all the horses.

Surprise Invitation

'My lord, I'm afraid our departure this morning may be delayed more than we had anticipated,' Norton said as he placed a cup of coffee on the bedside table.

'Oh? How so?'

'Although all the horses were supposedly released into the meadow adjacent to the stables last night, it seems that not all of the horses are to be found there this morning.'

James frowned.

'I suppose they ran off in a panic last night and could be anywhere. I take it one of ours is missing?'

'Two of ours, two of Lady Collins's and a riding horse belonging to another gentleman.'

'Good heavens. So many? Has the meadow no fence?'

'I believe, sir, the suggestion is that the fire was no accident but set deliberately by horse thieves. If the horses cannot be found somewhere nearby, that may well be the case.'

'Well, this is the last thing I need. Help me get dressed and down to breakfast. Then go and see what is happening now and if the horses have been found.'

By the time James got down to the private parlour for breakfast, the others were already there.

'Lady Collins, may I suppose you have heard about the missing horses?'

'Yes, indeed. All the grooms are out scouring the countryside for them. I have heard a suggestion of horse thieves and the landlord said the local magistrate has been called.'

James shook his head in despair.

'It is all very annoying and heaven only knows how long it will all take to sort out. Considering the short daylight hours at the moment and the cloudy weather too, I fear we may have to stay an extra night.'

Sarah and Helen looked at each other with wide eyes. Miss Trellis frowned. Amy didn't appear to care one way or another as she passed a cup of coffee to her employer.

'A small inn like this only has facilities for feeding and watering horses that arrive,' James continued. 'They don't have horses to exchange as they do at the stagecoach stops. I'm not sure what we'll do if the horses cannot be found.'

'We shall have to see what transpires,' Emma said. 'I continued on to Sawtry for its peace and quiet instead of stopping at Stilton where all the inns are noisy, but now I am starting to regret it. If my carriage horses are not found I shall have to secure replacements to complete my journey. At least in Stilton it would have been easy to find the extra horses at the big coaching inns.

'I may have to take the stage or the mail here in Sawtry and send a groom back from London. He can bring horses from my brother to collect my carriage. Or I suppose my coachman could go to Stilton, but they may refuse if he has no horses to exchange. It's all very complicated and a great nuisance.' Emma sighed deeply and shook her head in exasperation.

'Do we need to send a message to Lord Collins to say that you may be delayed?'

'No, it is not necessary. The present Lord Collins is my late husband's cousin and is not expecting me. I am now the Dowager Lady Collins. My husband was with the Ninety-fifth Regiment of Foot and died at the battle of Badajoz, a year ago last spring.'

'Excuse me, my commiserations. It was a careless question. I do beg your pardon.'

Emma shook her head slightly and waved away his apology.

'Do not concern yourself. I am on my way to visit my brother in London, but if it is only an extra day, he's not going to worry.'

James was thoughtful as he drank another cup of coffee. Lady Collins was very young to be a dowager and a widow. He supposed the war with France had created very many young widows. The widows of ordinary soldiers must have difficult lives. At least this one appeared to be comfortably situated, although for all he knew, the carriage and coachman were not hers, but belonged to the current Lord Collins.

However, if he had to spend a day here kicking his heels, he wouldn't mind having Lady Collins for company. She was quite lovely and a congenial companion so far.

He was a widower and she was a widow, so propriety was not much of an issue. They also had his two daughters, their nurse, governess and her maid as chaperones which was vastly more than was necessary.

James didn't really mind the enforced rest, for he was in no great hurry to spend another day cooped up in a travelling carriage with two fidgeting girls and their dour governess. At least the nursemaid could definitely go with his valet this time.

James thought it over as he sipped his coffee. Maybe there was another arrangement, whereby he could enjoy her company a little longer and also make the journey less tedious . . .

'Lady Collins, I suspect our horses will not be found, and if not, perhaps there is an alternative to condemning you to the stage. We definitely have two horses which will be sufficient for one of my carriages. Why do you not come with myself and my daughters to my mother's house in Baldock? It's less than a day's travel, so we will not need to stop overnight again.

'We are on our way there for her birthday. She can then send a groom back here with enough horses to rescue both our remaining carriages and take them down to Baldock.

'My mother will undoubtedly be happy for you to stay for a couple of nights while the carriages are retrieved. You can then go from her house down to London in your own carriage with borrowed horses and subsequently her groom can return from London to Baldock with those same horses.

'This will save you at least a day, if not two, waiting for replacement horses from London and also save you from travelling on the stage, which is surely less than comfortable.'

Emma cocked her head and studied him while she thought it over. He seemed to be respectable and this was definitely not a situation of his making. They had his two daughters as chaperones, and they would be travelling in broad daylight. Whilst she would not want to endanger her reputation, she was a widow, not an unmarried débutante, and besides, they were not likely to meet anyone known to her. Could this alternative work?

'Your vehicle will be impossibly crowded with seven of us, my lord, even assuming that your valet travels on the box.'

'I propose that Miss Trellis take the stage from here all the way to London where she may start her holiday early.'

Miss Trellis brightened at the prospect.

Sarah and Helen looked at each other, also brightening at the prospect.

'Your maid, Amy and Norton my valet could all take the stage to Baldock where I will arrange for them to be collected.

Norton is quite capable of guiding the group of servants. There are so many stagecoaches travelling past here and down the Great North Road through Baldock, I doubt it will be difficult to find places for them all. Thus there will only be four of us in my carriage and this should make it quite comfortable.'

Emma still had doubts about turning up at a stranger's house and expecting to be accommodated during a family gathering. He might think it a good idea, but if his mother didn't like it, Emma could be very embarrassed and uncomfortable.

'Are you quite sure your mother will not mind an unknown and unexpected guest for a couple of days? Especially if her house is filled with family members arriving for her birthday.'

James smiled.

'No, absolutely not. There is plenty of room and one more amongst us will be no difficulty. Besides, living on her own she is always happy to see fresh faces.'

'In that case, thank you, my lord, I

accept,' Emma said. She noted that if she was living on her own in the New Year, there would probably come a day when she would be glad to see a fresh face, too.

James felt unexpectedly pleased that Lady Collins had accepted his proposal and was going to be with them for a few days. He noticed that his daughters also looked very pleased at the plan.

He wondered, not for the first time, if he should send Miss Trellis off with an excellent reference and find a replacement with whom his daughters were more comfortable.

'Lady Collins,' Sarah said, 'if we are to be here all day, do you suppose you could tell us another story?'

'Sarah,' her father interrupted, 'if we are to be without Miss Trellis for several extra weeks, I think you two should spend today having a lesson from her.'

Sarah's and Helen's faces fell.

'My lord,' Emma said, 'I think you and I will be busy with the magistrate and the grooms this morning. Perhaps, if Miss Trellis says the girls are diligent with their lessons in the meantime, they may take me for a walk this afternoon? Assuming of course that all horses have been removed from the meadow and it does not rain.'

'Oh yes, please, Papa. We promise to study very hard this morning,' Sarah said, and Helen nodded her agreement excitedly.

James pursed his lips as he considered the proposal.

'It is very obliging of you, Lady Collins,' he said, 'but there is no need to trouble yourself like this.'

'It is no trouble at all and I'm sure I shall be glad of the exercise. No doubt the servants will be busy re-packing and rearranging all the baggage in order to suit the new plan.'

James bowed his thanks.

'Very well,' he said to the girls, 'but I shall expect a glowing report from Miss Trellis at luncheon and you must be on your best behaviour this afternoon.'

A Breath of Fresh Air

In the afternoon, after luncheon, Miss Trellis, Amy, Molly and Norton occupied themselves sorting out the baggage to suit the new plan. Emma set off with the two girls to walk down into the village, which was set back half a mile from the Great North Road. The meadow by the inn had been ruled out for a walk as it was occupied by cows and the main road also had too much traffic.

Emma was pleased to have an opportunity for a walk after spending too long this morning with the magistrate, who was very long-winded and liked to hear himself talk.

She was also grateful to have a fur-lined cloak and muff as the wind, while not strong, was bitterly cold. Thank goodness the road was lined by hedges to give a little shelter.

The girls didn't seem bothered by the cold or the wind as they skipped along happily in woollen capes and woollen mittens. Emma was grateful for their company, as it would have been improper and inadvisable for her to walk down this road on her own. She wouldn't have wanted to drag her maid with her, as she knew Molly would have been miserable. Molly had many merits, but was not an outdoors sort of girl and did not care for large amounts of fresh air.

There wasn't a great deal for the girls to see or do at this time of year as the trees and hedges had lost all their leaves and the only flowers were an occasional dandelion. Then there was a limit to how much interest could be found in rose hips and the plentiful small brown birds. Nevertheless, the girls seemed to be happy to be out and about.

'Sarah, Helen, are you warm enough?'

'Oh, yes, thank you, Lady Collins,' Sarah said, who was the older of the two and nearly always seemed to be their spokesman.

'Do tell me if you get cold or if you want to go back.'

'Oh, no, I don't want to go back yet,

thank you, walking with you is much nicer. Are you warm enough yourself, Lady Collins?'

'Yes, I am, thank you, Sarah. My cloak, muff and bonnet are all very warm.' Emma supposed that their lesson this morning must have been terribly dreary if it was much nicer to be walking in a bitterly cold wind with someone they hardly knew. She also appreciated that Sarah was thoughtful enough to enquire after Emma's comfort.

The more she saw of these two girls, the more she liked them.

They soon arrived in the centre of the village, which was mostly composed of thatched cottages but with a surprising number of public houses for such a small village. Emma surmised they catered for a large number of labourers from the surrounding farms. In any case, there wasn't much of interest for two small girls.

'Is there no duck pond on the village green?' Sarah asked.

'It's just grass,' Helen added in a voice filled with scorn.

'Never mind,' Emma said, 'let's go up this road. I see there is a windmill.'

The windmill proved to be of temporary interest. The brisk wind meant the sails were moving at full speed, but having watched them for several minutes, the girls observed that nothing much else seemed to be going on. Emma supposed the cold wind was sufficient to persuade the miller to stay inside with the door closed.

A farmer striding down the road with his dog was enough to divert the girls' attention, but after both girls had greeted the dog, the farmer called it to heel, tugged his forelock to Emma and carried on to wherever he was going. The delights of the village thus exhausted, Emma steered them all back towards the inn on the Great North Road.

James had sat on the bench outside the inn where he was sheltered from the wind and wistfully watched them go. His two darling daughters walking hand in hand with a beautiful young lady.

Perhaps, he thought, his mother was

right and it was time he found himself a wife. But who would marry a cripple like him who already had two growing daughters?

No doubt he could find some lady in London who would be attracted by his fortune and a chance to become a countess, but it wasn't enough.

While he would like someone who could care for him, at least a little, it was vital they be a loving mother to his girls. This someone would have to not mind living in very rural Rutland either, since he didn't often visit London. Ideally it would also be someone he could care for, too. He didn't need a beautiful face, but he did need a beautiful heart.

Well before the light started to fade, he saw the three of them walking back up the lane to the inn, hand in hand again. The girls waved to him. He waved back. Lady Collins said something to them and they ran the rest of the way to him while she continued walking.

'Papa,' Helen said breathlessly, 'there's a windmill and we saw the sails going around and around!'

'And there's a village green, but it's not very good,' Sarah said.

'Not very good? Why not?' James asked.

'Because it's just grass. There's no pond and no ducks, either.'

'I see. That is disappointing, isn't it? Never mind, we'll get to Grandmother's house tomorrow and she has a lake with ducks and swans on it.'

'Lady Collins,' an excited Sarah said, as Emma arrived, 'when we get to grandmother's house we'll take you to see the lake. It has ducks and swans on it.'

'I shall look forward to it,' Emma said with an indulgent smile. 'Now I think you should go in and find Amy or Miss Trellis. It must be time for your afternoon tea.'

The two girls scampered into the inn and Emma joined James on the bench.

'There wasn't a great deal to see in the village, but I think we all needed the exercise and fresh air,' she said.

'I am very much obliged to you, Lady Collins, I wish I could have taken them

41

myself. Unfortunately my horse was shot from under me in the Battle of Sahagun in 1808. It was a famous victory for the Hussars, but I fell awkwardly and then the horse fell on me, too. I broke my legs in several places and the bones were set badly amid the hurried retreat to Corunna. I have had difficulty walking ever since.'

Emma was a little surprised that he was offering this explanation to her, who was a stranger to him.

'It seems, then, we both have reason to resent Napoleon, but at least you came home, for which your family must be grateful.'

'You must think me selfish, to be speaking like this when you lost your husband.'

'No, not at all. You have suffered more misfortune than I have,' Emma put her hand on his sleeve. 'After all, you lost your wife, too.'

'Yes, she became ill and died two years ago. We all felt the loss, especially Sarah who is that bit older.'

They both fell into a reflective silence. Emma thought it was nice to talk to someone who had no ulterior motive of any kind and with whom she could relax. It was easy to talk to him, too, as if they had known each other for years. Even the current silence felt companionable.

'I suppose,' Emma said after a while, 'you are a younger son if you went off to join the army.'

'I was, but my older brother died of a fever last year, so I unexpectedly became the earl. Naturally I had sold out long before, when I was injured, so at least I didn't need to be recalled.'

'Is there no end to your troubles?'

James shrugged his shoulders, as if to say there was little he could do about it.

'At least I have two daughters whom I love dearly and they are a constant joy to me.'

'Yes, they are both delightful,' Emma said, thinking of their constant chatter during their walk.

'No doubt their grandmother will be overjoyed to see them,' James said, 'and they are certainly looking forward to seeing her and their cousins, too. They need other children to play with.'

Emma nodded agreement, remembering the times she used to play with her older brother Lionel. Sometimes he would bring some friends home during the school holidays too. Her husband Peter had been one of those friends.

'If you were in the cavalry, I suppose you enjoyed riding. Can you still ride?'

'Yes, but not for long, as I tire quickly. It really needs to be my own horse, too, who is used to me now. I had thought of bringing him, but decided not to, as there seemed little point in town. At least, when I am at home, it means I can get around on my own to see to the estate.'

James wondered why he was telling her all these things when he hardly knew her and they would soon part company. However, she was comfortable to be with and it was a relief to have someone to talk to who wasn't an employee, tenant or neighbour.

'Lady Collins, will you join me for

dinner this evening?'

'Gladly. I took dinner on a tray last night as I was very tired. Since we are to spend a couple of days together, please call me Emma. I think we can dispense with formality in private.' She turned to look at James with a raised eyebrow.

He bowed his head slightly in agreement.

'Thank you, Emma, I shall be pleased to have some informal company and perhaps you could call me James? In the meantime, let us go back inside before we both freeze to death out here.'

Journey Into the Unknown

The next morning they climbed into the earl's travelling carriage, Emma and James facing forward and the two girls with their backs to the horses. Emma thought the girls looked very happy to be travelling, not at all like the grumpy, fractious children the earl had described when Emma had arrived at the inn.

'I have in mind to stop at Sandy for luncheon and then we should be at Baldock by mid-afternoon, if that is agreeable to you,' James said as they moved out on to the Great North Road.

'Perfectly. I didn't relish staying in Sawtry for four days until my brother's horses arrived from London. It's an agreeable little inn, but there's nothing to do here. I suppose I could have gone on by mail coach, but this is much more comfortable.'

Emma observed the way James was sitting in the corner to make a little more room for his legs.

'My lord, you don't look very comfortable. Why sit across the front seat so that you can stretch your legs? The girls can come and sit either side of me.'

'Thank you, my lady, but the three of you would be squashed together.'

'No, not at all, I think we might be perfectly cosy,' Emma said. 'What do you think, girls?'

Both girls nodded agreement.

'There you are, my lord, so let us change over.'

Sarah and Helen stood while James moved across and then they sat either side of Emma. They all busied themselves rearranging the travelling blankets. The weather wasn't especially cold today, but hot bricks didn't last long.

'Lady Collins,' Sarah said, once they were comfortable, 'do we have to look for sheep?'

'Er, no, not unless you want to. Is there a reason to look out for sheep?'

'Miss Trellis is always telling us to look out of the window for sheep,' Sarah replied.

'She doesn't know what else to tell us to do,' Helen added innocently, 'but it's boring.'

It seems to me, Emma thought, that Miss Trellis is a singularly unimaginative governess.

'We have sheep on the farm in Spalding,' she said, 'but I have to admit I find it difficult to get enthusiastic about sheep.' She looked at James who seemed to be puzzled at the turn in the conversation. 'Do you get excited about sheep, my lord?'

The girls giggled at the question.

'I am interested in sheep, as I am interested in everything on the estate and we have a lot of sheep, but excited? No, I am afraid not,' he replied with a mock serious face. 'How about cows, Lady Collins, do you find cows enchanting?'

Emma put a finger to her lips and frowned as she pretended to consider the matter.

'Well, to be honest, I don't find them very . . . thrilling. Most of the time they seem to be standing around chewing grass.' She pulled a silly face and made exaggerated chewing motions with her mouth.

The girls burst out laughing and James started chuckling as well.

'Oh, Lady Collins, I'm so glad you came with us instead of . . . ' Sarah's voice petered out as her father gave her a meaningful look.

'Tell me, my lord,' Emma asked, to move past the awkward moment, 'are you now more comfortable, sitting like that?'

'Yes, I am, thank you. I don't know why I didn't try this before.'

'Good. Now, girls, why don't you tell me a little about your grandmother's house and the people I shall be meeting? The house and everyone in it will be new to me, so should I be a little scared?'

'Oh no, Lady Collins,' Sarah said anxiously as she took hold of Emma's arm. 'You needn't, oh . . . you're teasing me! No, you won't be frightened with Papa, Helen and me to look after you.'

'Lady Collins,' Helen said a little timidly, 'do you know any more stories?'

James rolled his eyes and shook his head gently in resignation.

'Well, let me see,' Emma said. 'Shall I tell you the one about the sleeping beauty?'

James settled back into the corner of the carriage to listen to the story, too. She had told the story at Sawtry in a very entertaining way. He was warm and comfortable. Emma's voice was very soothing and his eyelids began to droop. Very soon he was fast asleep.

A little later he woke up when he felt his cheek being kissed. He blinked and came fully awake to the sound of two small girls giggling uncontrollably.

'Oh, at last, the handsome prince is awake — your kisses did the trick,' Emma said.

Sarah and Helen roared with laughter as their father looked around in confusion.

'Very good, my lord, you played the part of the sleeping beauty to perfection.'

James quickly understood he had fallen asleep during the telling of 'Sleeping Beauty'. However, he was amused by the situation and grinned sheepishly at Emma.

She responded with a broad smile.

James thought that when she smiled like that, there was no doubt she was a very beautiful woman and he was very lucky to have her company on what could otherwise be an exceedingly tiresome journey. He must have been very comfortable and relaxed to have fallen asleep as he had.

The carriage slowed down and turned into the inn on the outskirts of Sandy. Emma left the carriage first so that she and the coachman could help James get down. Then Emma and James led the way in to the inn and to a parlour.

Once they were all seated and had been served with tea, cakes, ale and lemonade, Emma turned to James.

'James,' she said quietly, 'I hope you didn't mind me helping you down from the carriage. I know it is usually the gentleman who helps the lady down.'

'I've had to get used to being helped these days. It is a little humiliating, but it's better than falling on my face in the dirt.'

Emma put her hand on his arm.

'There is nothing to be ashamed of, you know. Everybody can see that you have been injured and anybody with any sense can guess that it happened while you were defending them from Napoleon.

'I expect that many of them would be glad to rush forward and lend a hand but they don't, because they think you would be embarrassed and resent it.'

James didn't know what to say. He had never thought of it in those terms. He had always felt like a child who needed help with the smallest things. He patted her hand as it laid on his sleeve.

'The only thing to be ashamed of here,' Emma said, looking at the cup in front of her, 'is this tea. It is perfectly dreadful. I think I shall ring for more lemonade instead.'

Once the horses and hot bricks had been changed, the cakes consumed and the drinks finished, they climbed back into the coach which then returned on to the Great North Road and headed south for Baldock.

The rest of the journey was filled companionably by the sisters telling Emma all about their family and about grandmother's house and about the lake and about the stables, with James adding the occasional word of explanation.

Just Good Friends

As predicted, they arrived at the dowager countess's house just outside Baldock by mid-afternoon. It was a house with extensive gardens but without any attached estate, Emma had been told by James. As the carriage rumbled down the gravelled drive, the girls were clearly excited and Emma looked at the house with interest. She could see the house was substantial and understood James's assertion that his mother had plenty of space for unexpected guests.

The gardens were well tended, although looking a little barren in late November. The grass was neatly scythed, but there were scattered brown leaves which had been blown here and there.

They pulled up at the base of the horseshoe steps, the front door opened and a couple of footmen hurried down. Emma and the girls left the carriage first and then waited as the footmen steadied James on the step and handed him his walking sticks.

As they all slowly mounted to the front door, an older lady appeared in the doorway.

'Go along, you two,' James said to the girls. 'Go and greet your grandmother.'

The girls ran up the remaining steps to where their grandmother embraced them, said something quietly and released them. They raced off further into the house. James's mother straightened up and looked with interest at Emma, then at the carriage and then back to James.

'Mother,' he said, 'before you ask, and before you jump to any rash conclusions, allow me to present Lady Collins to you, whom we met on our journey. Lady Collins, may I present my mother the Dowager Countess Benfield.'

Emma had noticed Lady Benfield's scrutiny of her and was glad his lordship forestalled any misunderstandings before he had a chance to explain everything.

'Watson,' James said, addressing the butler, 'would you ask the housekeeper to make up a guest room for Lady Collins, please.'

'Yes, my lord,' he said as he collected their hats, coats and gloves.

'And have tea sent up to the drawing-room as well,' the dowager added. They made their way slowly up the stairs. 'Lady Collins,' she said, as they followed James, 'would you like to refresh yourself, before we have tea?'

Emma recognised that her hostess was being tactful and giving her an excuse to absent herself in case her son needed to explain anything indelicate. However, since there was no cause for embarrassment, there was only one thing on her mind.

'Thank you, Lady Benfield, but I am positively dying for a decent cup of tea. The one they gave me in the inn at Sandy was quite dreadful and I couldn't finish it.'

'Lady Collins,' James said, without turning his head, 'I am gaining the impression that you cannot function without a constant supply of tea.'

'Alas,' Emma said, 'my principal vice

is revealed.'

The dowager glanced speculatively between the two of them.

By the time they reached the drawing-room, the tea tray was already there, as James's progress up the stairs was very slow.

'Now then, James,' his mother said, once they were all seated and each had a cup of tea, 'where is your other carriage and where, for that matter, is your valet, Miss Trellis, the girl's nursemaid and Lady Collins's maid too?'

'My valet should be escorting the maids to a coaching inn in Baldock and my coach should now be on its way to collect them. Miss Trellis has been given leave for an early start to her Christmas holiday with her family in London. However, let me begin at the beginning in Sawtry . . . ' He explained the situation. 'So this is why I am foisting an unexpected guest upon you in the person of Lady Collins,' he added.

'I do hope this is not inconvenient for you,' Emma said, feeling uncomfortable, 'but I was tempted by his lordship's offer when I compared it with taking the stage to London or staying at Sawtry for several days.'

'Oh, no,' the dowager said, 'you have done absolutely right. It is no problem at all, you are very welcome, I have plenty of space and I always like to meet someone new. I shall introduce you to my daughter and her husband as soon as they return from their walk around the grounds.'

Just then there was a thunder of many small feet on the stairs which stopped suddenly just outside the drawing-room. There was then the sound of whispering and the three of them in the drawing-room looked towards the door expectantly. The door opened slowly and there was a procession of four small children.

'Good afternoon, Uncle James,' a boy, who was a head taller than the other three, said. He bowed, his younger brother followed suit and James nodded to them.

'Good afternoon, Robert. Good afternoon, David,' James said. Clearly the boys had been instructed to be on their best formal behaviour. 'May I make known to you Lady Collins,' he continued, and the boys bowed to Emma who nodded in return.

'Good afternoon, Lady Collins. Sarah says you tell wonderful stories,' Robert said. 'Could you tell us one later, please?'

'One about knights and dragons would be best,' David added.

'Boys, boys, you mustn't pester Lady Collins,' the exasperated dowager said, 'she's not here to tell you stories and besides, she's only just arrived and hasn't even finished her tea.'

The children looked crestfallen and Emma couldn't resist their disappointment.

'Perhaps later, at your bedtime, I could tell you one?'

The children brightened up instantly.

'However, I don't think I know one about knights, but there is one called 'The Princess and the Dragon'. It has a brave prince and perhaps he would do instead of the knight?'

'Oh, yes, please, Lady Collins, thank you very, very much,' Robert replied. He seemed to have become the leader and spokesman of their little band.

'Now then, children,' the dowager said, 'it's time you went up to the nursery to inspect your parents' old toys which are still up there somewhere.'

Four excited children scampered out and raced down the hallway.

'Perhaps I should explain,' James said to his mother. 'The girls have discovered that Lady Collins is a storyteller par excellence. Now they are constantly asking her to tell them stories.' He turned towards Emma. 'I am afraid, Lady Collins, that you have made a rod for your own back. Your only solution now is to take a firm line and refuse, otherwise they will pester you endlessly.'

'I really don't mind. I have no children of my own and my nephews are getting a little too old for the stories. At least, they pretend they are too old and say they are only agreeing for the sake of the youngest.

'He, of course, insists that he is too old as well, but he doesn't insist for very long. My only worry is that I shall run out of stories, but since I will only be here for a day or so, it seems unlikely.'

Just then, James's sister Katherine and her husband, Victor, Baron Weston, came into the room. They hesitated slightly in the doorway at the unexpected sight of a stranger taking tea. Another round of introductions and explanations then followed and very soon it was time to change for dinner.

'Victor,' the dowager said, 'be so good as to ring the bell please before you go.'

As Victor and Katherine left the room, Norton and the housekeeper appeared quickly, having anticipated that they would be needed. The housekeeper took Emma to her room, while Norton was told by Lady Benfield to wait outside a moment.

'James,' she said, 'I am pleasantly surprised by Lady Collins, but a little confused, too. Exactly what are your intentions towards her?'

'Intentions? None. We have been thrown into each other's company by chance and we chose the most expeditious way out of our difficulties. Beyond this, nothing.'

'I see. Nothing more?'

'No, and before you get ideas, she is only just out of mourning and has no plans to remarry. Furthermore, even if she did have such plans, she could easily do so much better than me. She is a very attractive woman in the prime of life, genteel and with an impeccable background.'

'Hmm, if you say so.' She studied James for a moment, who remained impassive. Was James protesting just a little too much? She rose to her feet. 'We should get changed.'

Close Harmony

Emma was shown to her room by the housekeeper to find her maid had arrived and already unpacked their bags. Molly had a jug of hot water to hand and had laid out a suitable dress for the evening.

'Did you have long to wait in Baldock?' Emma asked, as Molly undid the buttons down the back of the day gown.

'No, my lady, and his lordship's valet Mr Norton was very attentive. He made sure we got down at the right place and ordered refreshments while we waited for his lordship's carriage to collect us.'

'Did Miss Trellis continue on the same stagecoach to London?'

'No, my lady, she got one before ours, but there wasn't room in it for all four of us. I think she was very content to go on her own without us.

'She seemed to think a governess was too good to associate with a valet and lady's maid, never mind a nursemaid.'

Molly sniffed in disdain.

Emma nodded, as her opinion was similar.

'She did appear to be a bit humourless and the girls don't seem to like her much, either. Perhaps she's come down in the world and resents it.'

Molly shrugged as if she didn't care one way or the other.

Once Emma was wearing an evening gown, she turned each way in front of the mirror to check that it fell properly. For some obscure reason she felt she needed to look her best for dinner.

Be that as it may, the first thing she needed to do, was go to the nursery and tell the children the promised story. When she had left for London, they would probably remember her only vaguely as a lady who told them stories, but in the meantime it was nice to feel wanted.

★　★　★

After dinner, the ladies retired to the drawing-room. The dowager sat next to

Emma while her daughter occupied herself with the tea tray.

'Lady Collins, you are going down to London, is that right?'

'Yes, I shall stay with my brother and his family for a month while I decide what to do.'

'Decide what to do?'

'They have invited me to live with them.' Emma sighed. 'They are perfectly nice people but I might feel that I'm under their feet all the time and that wouldn't be at all comfortable for any of us.'

'I thought you had a house in Spalding?'

'I do and I don't. The house with the estate was entailed and now belongs to my late husband's cousin. He is planning to move there at Easter.

'He has kindly offered me the use of the dower house, as is right and proper, but I'm not sure that is a good idea, either. The house is several miles outside the town and I might feel isolated in the dower house. At least in London there will be more society, although I don't know anybody there yet.'

'I see. It is an awkward position in which to find oneself.'

'It is, because I have no other close family, nor am I in a position to set up my own establishment in London, for example. It may be a difficult choice, but I'm thankful I do have a choice.'

'Do you not think to remarry? You are still young and have kept your looks.'

Emma smiled at the compliment.

'I have no plans to marry again and I haven't given it any thought. I'm only just out of mourning and besides, I have precious little to bring to a marriage.

'While my jointure is not large, it is sufficient to run a small household at the dower house, so I have no particular need to marry.'

The dowager was about to reply when the door opened and the two gentlemen joined them. Victor went to join his wife, while James made a beeline for the piano.

Emma watched him with curiosity. It was usually the ladies of the house who played piano, not the gentlemen.

The dowager noticed Emma watching her son.

'He's very good, you know. While he was recuperating from his injuries he was bored to tears. One day he took it into his head to learn to play the piano.

'Other men might have spent their leisure time shooting or fishing, but both pastimes would have been difficult for him. Instead he spent his leisure time practising the piano. He spent hours and hours practising.

'He has always wanted to be the best at whatever he does. It was because he was so good on a horse that he joined the Hussars. It was literally the epitome of pride coming before a fall.

'He is more humble now and probably the better for it, although I sometimes wonder if he has gone too far the other way. He needs to value himself more.'

James started to play and his small audience fell silent to listen. Emma rapidly realised that his mother had been correct.

He was not only technically very

correct, but he managed to put some feeling into his playing too. As he finished the piece, they all applauded and he appeared pleased with his efforts as well. He looked at Emma.

'Lady Collins, do you sing?'

'Sing? I used to, but I haven't done so for some time. It would not have been appropriate while I was in mourning, would it?'

'Can I persuade you to join me? We have a wide selection of music and songs to choose from. We are bound to find something that suits you.'

'Well, I . . .'

'Oh, Lady Collins, do let us hear you,' the dowager said, 'there are only a handful of us here, so it couldn't possibly be considered improper and you are out of mourning now anyway.

'I have to say the rest of us sing like frogs, so anything you can do must be an improvement.'

Emma laughed and went to stand beside James. They quickly selected a traditional country ballad. James played the introduction and looked up at Emma as she started singing, as he knew the music by heart, just as Emma knew the words. Emma had a clear alto voice and when they got to the chorus, James harmonised with his tenor. As they sang they smiled and looked into each other's eyes.

The other three had smiles that reached from ear to ear, which one could suppose was merely appreciation of the singing rather than suspicion of something else.

After another two songs, the dowager rose to her feet.

'Well, my dears, that was quite lovely, but I am afraid I have had a busy day and am rather tired. Tomorrow will no doubt be just as busy, with an early start, so I shall retire now.' She turned to Emma.

'Tomorrow is my birthday and in the evening we shall have a few of my friends for dinner.'

'I expect my carriage will be here by the afternoon, so I will be out of your way by then,' Emma said, 'otherwise I will be upsetting your arrangements.'

'No, no, I won't hear of it, you must stay at least until the following day,' the dowager said, 'in fact, you are welcome to stay as long as you like. I'm sure we will all be happy with your company.'

'You are very kind,' a flustered Emma said, 'but my brother must already be wondering what has delayed me.'

'The offer stands, my dear Lady Collins,' the dowager said, patting Emma's arm, 'but now I must be off to bed.'

There was general agreement for an early night, and as they filed out of the room, James's valet appeared in case he needed steadying on the stairs.

An Attractive Proposition

The next morning, as Emma was leaving the breakfast room, the four children appeared, with Amy hovering behind them.

'Excuse me, Lady Collins,' Sarah said, 'but we said yesterday we would show you the swans and ducks on the lake. Would you like to see them now?'

'That would be lovely,' Emma replied, impressed by the polite, decorous behaviour of the children, 'but it looks chilly outside. We should all put on some coats and gloves.'

'Yes!' all the children cried, before they thundered up the stairs towards the nursery.

'Children, you mustn't run in the house,' Amy called faintly as she followed them. They were too excited and paid absolutely no attention to their nursemaid.

Emma watched them go. It wasn't her place to correct them and in any case she was pleased to see them so happy.

'I'm sorry if my daughters are badgering you again,' a deep male voice behind her said.

Emma turned to face James who was making his way slowly out of the breakfast room.

'Oh, no,' she said, 'they are delightful, I enjoy their company immensely. I imagine my nephews will seem dull by comparison. They are that much older and probably won't be very interested in an aunt. We are going to visit the ducks on the lake. Will you join us?'

James looked pointedly at his legs and walking sticks.

Emma thought it would be a shame if his disability stopped him enjoying the company of his children when the girls went outside. She was sure she would enjoy it more as well, if he came with her.

'Pah! It's not far and we are in no hurry. I am a guest here and I feel the need of a gentleman's arm to support me among strangers.'

James studied her for a moment as he considered the idea.

'Watson!' he called out to the butler, who was surely somewhere within hailing distance. 'Tell my valet to bring my coat and boots.'

Emma's face broke into a grin.

'I shall be back as soon as I have my boots on, and my cloak and bonnet.'

Soon afterwards, Emma and James were walking very slowly across the lawn towards a bench facing the lake. Ahead of them were four chattering children dancing around, followed by Amy clutching a large cloth bag of dried bread.

Beyond them was the lake where two swans and a flock of ducks were swimming quickly towards the children in anticipation of being fed.

A breeze was cooling everybody's faces and the sky threatened cold rain before long, but James was happy despite his now aching legs. He enjoyed having a pretty lady hanging on his arm and it felt almost as if he had his whole family again. It was a feeling that he had almost forgotten.

Strangely, it would be good, he thought, to have a wife who would chivvy him along, as Emma had done a few minutes ago. It was too easy to stay sitting in the same place all day.

Yes, he knew Emma wasn't his wife and never would be, even if she changed her mind about remarrying. Once she got over her bereavement, she could do so much better for herself than him, but regardless, the feeling of rightness persisted and he decided to enjoy it while he could.

His mother was correct, and he should look around for a wife. How he would find one who was prepared to take on two boisterous and growing daughters, as well as a crippled husband, was another matter entirely.

There must surely be some lady left on the shelf, and without prospects, who would view it as a reasonable bargain. He could offer a comfortable and respectable life as a countess, which had to be an attractive position for somebody. As long as she had a pleasant personality and was of good family he could accept a marriage of convenience, too.

They reached a wooden bench and sat down after checking to make sure it was reasonably dry. James watched the children. It was good for them to spend time with their cousins who were near enough in age for the difference to not matter. His girls were animated and clearly happy here.

He wondered if it was the absence of Miss Trellis, the presence of their cousins or perhaps even the influence of Lady Collins. He turned to look at her as she watched the children feeding the waterfowl.

'The girls seem so relaxed and free here,' James said. 'I am wondering if it is their cousins or because Miss Trellis has been depressing them.'

'I'm not in a position to judge. I met all of you just a few days ago and the girls seemed happy to me. They were scared the night of the fire, but it was not surprising, was it? I dare say everyone was a bit on edge and nervous that night.

'However, it did seem to me they were not fond of Miss Trellis nor she of them.

Has she been with you long?'

'About six months. The previous one was offered a position teaching the daughters of a duke, so not surprisingly, she took it. The duke and duchess were visiting for a weekend. I doubt I shall invite them again if they are going to steal my staff.'

Emma glanced at him with the glimmer of a smile on her lips.

'Miss Trellis came with an excellent reference from an agency, but I don't think her heart is in it,' James added.

'No doubt, if you decide to try someone else, you will also give Miss Trellis an excellent reference to speed her on her way.'

'Yes, and as you are suggesting, it might not be her first time, either.'

Finding a new governess would be tiresome, but it would be easier for him to do in London rather than in Oakham.

'The girls will miss you when you have gone to London,' he said, thinking how he would miss her as well.

'They are enchanting. I shall miss them too. I regret not having my own children, but our marriage was not long and we were often apart because of the army and the war. Life is like that sometimes and you simply have to play the cards that fate deals you. You must all call on me when you all go to town as well.'

'Will your brother not think it odd?'

Emma pondered the question for a moment.

'That I should receive a call from a widower with two small girls? No, I don't see why he should see it as any more than courtesy. By then I will have explained everything which has happened. I wonder if his three boys might like to go with your girls to Astley's Amphitheatre?'

'Astley's? I wasn't planning to go.'

'How on earth can a Hussar not take his children to see an equestrian show at Astley's?'

'Ex-Hussar. Because it's difficult and painful for me to get into and out of that sort of place.'

'Well I think it very poor spirited of you not to make the effort,' Emma said, waving her hand dismissively.

James looked at her in amazement. He was going to say something, but then just sat there with his mouth hanging open, not knowing what to say. How dare she reprimand him?

'And if you don't go with your girls,' Emma continued, 'then the boys probably won't go and then I will have no excuse to see it, either.'

James closed his mouth with a snap and turned to watch the children. Was she saying she wanted to spend the day with him and five children at an entertainment in London?

Surely she would be glad to have seen the back of them by then? She couldn't possibly want to spend the day with an invalid and two clinging children, never mind her three nephews.

'I have never been to Astley's, you know, and I've always wanted to,' Emma muttered.

It seemed she did definitely want to spend a day in London with him and a gaggle of children. James knew when he was beaten and, really and truly, didn't mind that he was being nagged and manipulated into agreeing to this outing. In fact, he found it to be an inviting prospect.

Yes, he should make the effort, if it meant spending the day with Emma and his girls.

Perhaps he could swallow his pride and let his valet help him more than usual to get around. He looked at Emma who was drawing breath to say more.

'All right, stop, stop, enough, we'll go,' James grumbled, pretending to be annoyed, 'otherwise I'll never hear the end of it.' He glanced again at Emma. She was now sitting there looking very smug and pleased with herself.

The children came over, since the bread was finally exhausted.

'Papa,' Sarah said, pointing at the ducks, 'that big duck kept grabbing all the bread so we had to throw some near the other ducks so they could get some too. Robert managed to throw some ever so far into the lake.'

Robert stood up straighter and looked pleased with himself.

'And when the swans got some bread, they wagged their tails,' Helen added.

'Uncle James,' Robert said, 'there is a litter of puppies in the stables. Would you like to see them?'

James weighed up the alternatives of hobbling across to the stables or of staying on the bench talking to Emma. It didn't take him long.

'I would love to, but not just at the moment. Perhaps tomorrow. Why not take your cousins to see them?'

'Come on, let's go,' David said, running across the grass towards the stables and the others raced after him.

They watched the children for a few moments and then again faced the lake where the ducks and swans were now dispersing.

'I do hope the puppies are all spoken for, or are very young,' James said.

'So it makes it impossible for the girls to take one home?'

'Precisely. It's not that I object to dogs but I don't fancy carrying one all the way back to Oakham in a crowded carriage.

We already have dogs on the Home Farm and if they really want one, it would make more sense to get one from there.'

'Will you have to harden your heart tomorrow if the girls fall in love with a puppy?'

'Probably. I shall have to ask Victor for his moral support tomorrow morning. Clearly I am susceptible to manipulation and coercion by pretty females.'

James glanced at Emma and saw that she was not fully able to suppress a grin.

'Do you have a house in London?' Emma asked after a quiet moment.

'I do, but it's let. I hardly ever visit and there was no point in it standing empty. We will go to London together with my sister and her family, then stay with them for a week or so.

'While I'm doing some business in the City, the girls can stay with their cousins. I shall take them out and about now and again, weather permitting and, of course to Astley's. I think I shall have to engage a new governess too. Then we will all come back here for Christmas. What are your plans?'

'I shall stay with my brother and his family over Christmas, do a little shopping and of course visit Astley's. Then early in the New Year I have to decide whether to make my home in London or go back to Spalding.'

They watched the waterfowl for a few minutes. A cold breeze was picking up and Emma shivered.

'This evening it will be a fairly small party,' James said. 'I understand Mother has invited three local couples and her old friend, the general. I suspect she is grateful for your presence, as you have conveniently evened up the numbers for her.'

Emma nodded gently.

'That makes me more comfortable — not that I mean your family hasn't made me very welcome. Will you play the piano for us after dinner?'

'I'm sure I will. I expect Mother will put some card tables out or roll up the carpet for a little dancing. I don't know what she has in mind.'

Emma shivered again, the cold was

penetrating now and a warm fireplace was calling her.

'Shall we go back into the house?'

Forgotten Feelings

The birthday dinner was a convivial affair. James sat at one end of the table as head of the family and the dowager sat at the other end as hostess. Emma was seated to James's right and beside Victor. All the other people around the table seemed to know each other, so conversation was lively and informal. The dishes selected were the dowager's favourites and since her tastes were fairly conventional, everybody else thought them agreeable, too.

Emma found Victor's conversation a little dull. Politics had never interested her much, but it seemed to be Victor's main reason for living in London. James's conversation was much more to her taste.

He described the small town of Oakham and Emma contrasted it with Spalding. They talked easily together and Emma felt a little regret and irritation when courtesy dictated she should turn back to talk to Victor.

At the end, the gentlemen didn't spend long on their port and cigars before joining the ladies. James made straight for the piano and Emma followed him.

'What do you intend to play for us, James?'

'I had nothing specific in mind. What is your preference?'

Emma smiled to herself. It was as if he was going to play something specifically for her, rather than for his mother, whose birthday it was.

'Something by Herr Beethoven perhaps, since we know he dislikes Napoleon as much as we both do.'

'Yes, a good choice. His sonata number six, I think, because it's not too long. Once the tea tray has been dealt with, Mother may have other plans, so something long wouldn't be appropriate. I don't know it by heart but I think it is in the stack over there if you could find it for me.' He pointed to a pile of sheet music on a nearby table.

Emma sorted through the stack until she found the music which she passed to

James.

As he was arranging it on the stand, the dowager called to her.

'Lady Collins, do come and sit with the general and myself,' she said and Emma went to join them on the sofa.

'I understand Captain Collins was in the Ninety-fifth Foot,' the general said. 'A fine regiment founded by my friend Colonel Massingham. He died in the retreat to Corunna, about the same time as young Benfield's accident,' the general said, nodding towards James.

'Too many good men lost due to the infernal Corsican's visions of grandeur.'

He lapsed into silence as James started to play, leaving Emma to reflect upon how many other lives had been destroyed or disrupted, not just of the soldiers but of their families, too.

Once James had finished playing, the servants appeared to clear away the tea things and roll up the carpet. The room was not very large for dancing, but since there were not many guests, it was not too important. While they all moved out of the way of the servants, Emma drifted back to the piano.

'That was very well played, James, you are very talented.'

'Careful now, Emma,' James said with a laugh, 'otherwise your compliments will go to my head and I shall become insufferable. I have been asked to play some waltzes. Do you waltz?'

'There was little call for it in Spalding and little opportunity with my husband being away so much. Now I am afraid I have lost all interest in dancing.'

'That is understandable. I wish I could ask you to waltz with me, but naturally it is out of the question.' He waved a hand at his legs with a wry smile. 'Anyway, who then would play the music?'

They exchanged sad smiles.

'Perhaps,' he said, 'you would sit with me under the guise of fetching music and turning pages?'

There was a second piano stool and Emma carried it over and placed it next to James. She was enjoying his company.

It was years since her husband had

gone off to war and now she had been widowed for well over a year. Loneliness had slowly crept up on her and there had been no children or nearby family to keep it at bay.

Having an attractive man pay her attention and invite her company was making her feel warm inside in a way that she had almost forgotten.

James was enjoying himself immensely, too, and not just with the music. He had a beautiful companion who was treating him like a friend.

These days, ladies generally fell into two camps. The first group were quite obviously insincere in their attentions and only interested in the prospect of becoming a wealthy countess. Not the grasping sort of character he would want to marry. The second group were full of pity for his disability and intensely irritating as a result.

Now at last he had a female friend who had no inclination to marry and merely chivvied him so as to not let his injury hold him back.

He needed to find someone who could be a friend, perhaps because they weren't actively hunting for a husband, and who would be good company for him.

He could see that he had been on his own for a little too long and was in danger of becoming a recluse. That wasn't good for him nor for his daughters.

But if such a lady wasn't looking for a husband, he would have to hope they might still agree to a proposal, given a little persuasion. It was a long time since he had courted a lady.

He wondered if Emma might be persuadable but quickly dismissed the idea. She definitely wasn't looking for a husband and someone like Emma could do so much better than him.

James played several waltzes and a country dance, but with only four dancing couples the choice was limited. His mother therefore decreed that James had played enough and it was time for cards. This had been anticipated, so the servants quickly set out three tables, chairs and cards.

'Emma,' James said, 'I do hope you play whist and you will do me the honour of being my partner.'

'I shall be delighted, especially if you are an expert, as I fear I am sadly mediocre.'

They exchanged warm smiles and James decided he didn't mind if they won or not, having Emma as his partner was pleasure enough. He wondered if she could be persuaded to linger a little longer before going off to London — even though he wouldn't be courting her.

A Very Unsuitable Match

The children lay in wait for the adults to finish breakfast. They were already dressed for the outdoors.

'Papa,' Sarah said, as soon as James left the breakfast room, 'will you come with us to see the puppies?'

James looked at the four expectant young faces. He was outnumbered and needed help.

'Very well,' he said, 'but Lady Collins must come, too. I'm sure she knows a great deal about puppies.'

Emma had followed him from the room. She raised her eyebrows and looked at James.

He smiled with false innocence as he was sure she wouldn't refuse. Forcing her to go out in the cold with them was revenge, too, as she had done the same to him yesterday.

'Very well, but I shall need to put on my cloak because it looks to be freezing out there,' Emma said.

Molly materialised behind the children.

She was holding the cloak. Emma gave her a questioning look but Molly just gave an apologetic little shrug.

James also noticed that his valet was hovering with his greatcoat, too, and wondered who the organiser was of this little expedition.

He narrowed his eyes at Robert, whom he guessed was the most likely candidate. His suspicions seemed confirmed when Robert's face broke into a broad grin.

Emma and James made their way slowly down to the stable block surrounded by four dancing and impatient chattering children.

They were led to a stall at the end, away from any draughts coming through the door. In one corner, in the middle of a generous amount of straw, was a black and white dog nursing five puppies.

The dog looked up at them warily, obviously decided all the people were not a threat and laid her head back down on the straw. The children had clearly been told not to disturb them when the puppies were being fed, but they stood and watched with rapt attention.

Fortunately, for James's peace of mind, the puppies were most likely less than a couple of weeks old.

'The puppies are very small,' James said, 'and they won't be ready to leave their mother for many weeks yet.'

However, as he surveyed the small adoring crowd surrounding the dogs, it struck James how this was so much like a family group, even though only the girls were his. The boys were sons of his sister. The motherly figure standing next to him was no relation at all. He was reminded that his heir was a second cousin whom he hadn't seen for very many years.

He added another item to his list of requirements in a wife. She needed to be willing and, hopefully, able to provide him with an heir and ideally a spare, not that this could be guaranteed. If the Fates were mischievous, he could find himself surrounded by daughters.

They slowly made their way back to the warmth of the house, while the children raced in a roundabout way to see if the ducks and swans had done anything exciting since yesterday.

'Why do you not stay an extra couple of days?' James asked. 'We all enjoy your company.' Of course, he really meant that he was enjoying her company.

'It is tempting,' she said. 'I said in my letter yesterday to my brother that I would arrive no later than tomorrow, and that seemed a bit pessimistic at the time. If I'm delayed any further he will start to worry and come looking for me. Besides, I do feel it is bit of an imposition on your mother.'

'Oh, my mother wouldn't mind at all.'

'Maybe not, but I still feel uncomfortable, as if I had been foisted on her.'

'Regardless, your carriage hasn't arrived yet. Even if it arrives this afternoon, it will be too late to set off for London. The horses will need to be rested and it gets dark very early at this time of year.'

As James knew all too well, the carriage could arrive at any moment this morning and there were two rested horses in the stables.

Departing after an early lunch was entirely feasible, as it was probably little more than 30 miles to her brother's house. It was a good road and no need to stop for meals. In fact, it need not take much over four hours, so she could be arriving as the sun was setting.

James thought Emma probably knew all this, and it was merely a question of whether or not she would seize the excuse.

'I suppose it would be sensible to wait for the carriage to get here before making definite plans.

'Assuming it arrives today, I can be all packed and ready to go by noon tomorrow. So, yes, I'll stay, but only until tomorrow, provided there is no difficulty when you tell your mother.'

James felt pleased that Emma had taken the excuse and was staying an extra day. He was confident his mother would not mind. If he was not much mistaken, his mother and Emma got on very well together.

'Let's ask her now, shall we?'

Time to Say Goodbye

The next morning, as James was leaving the breakfast room, he found Robert lurking just outside. James paused and looked at his nephew thoughtfully.

'Robert, what are you up to this morning?'

'Uncle James, we can see from the nursery windows that the lake is freezing over and we want to go and have a look. Amy says we must not go unless an adult goes with us to make sure we don't fall in.'

'I see,' James said, resting on his walking sticks, 'and why can Amy not go with you?'

'She says she wouldn't know what to do if we did fall in.'

James could see that Amy had a clear idea of her own limitations.

'I see. Can your parents not go with you?'

'No, Uncle, they say they are much too busy this morning and the ice will probably melt by this afternoon. They said I should ask you.'

James wondered what, exactly, was preoccupying Robert's parents? He had a deep suspicion his sister Katherine was devising a way to get him out of the house so as to get some exercise.

'What makes you think I will be of any help if you fall in, considering it's hard for me to walk?'

'I asked that and Mama says you know how to swim.'

James burst out laughing. He hadn't swum for years and the water would be ice cold. Katherine may have been literally correct, but not necessarily in any helpful way. She was obviously up to something. He noticed Robert's eyes flick to one side. James looked that way and saw that Emma had followed him out of the breakfast room like the day before.

'And then Helen said if Lady Collins would come, too, we would be perfectly safe,' Robert continued.

'What is this?' Emma asked.

'If you ask me,' James said, 'it is a

conspiracy. It seems that we are being manipulated to go down to the lake again this morning.'

'Feeding the ducks once more?'

'No, apparently to inspect ice on the surface of the lake. Not that I can see much point in the exercise.'

'Oh. Very well. We had better put our boots and warm clothing on in that case.'

James stared at Emma. Was she crazy? Wanting to go out in this freezing weather?

'Come along, my lord,' Emma said, 'don't dawdle or the ice may melt by the time you get there.'

They all went out very cautiously. The grass was covered in a hard frost and the paved path was slippery, so they walked on the grass. Robert and David quickly discovered they could slide on the grass and Sarah and Helen immediately joined in. Unfortunately, Helen instantly slipped over and started to cry. Emma picked her up and carried her as they walked slowly towards the lake.

'I don't like sliding on the grass,' Helen sniffled.

'No, you leave that to the others,' Emma said, wiping a little frosty grass from Helen's cheek. 'You and I will go to see what the ducks are doing. We shall go quite slowly because your father can't go fast and in any case, my boots are a bit slippery on this frosty grass.'

Helen beamed at Emma. It seemed the delight at being carried by her had erased all thoughts of falls and bruises.

When they arrived at the lake there was little to see except some optimistic swans and ducks swimming in their direction. The boys had been the ones keen to inspect the ice so James directed a warning to them.

'Robert, David,' James said, 'I want you to observe how the ice is only around the edges and around the rushes. Also, the ice looks black because it is thin. Nobody should go on the ice until it has frozen for several days and looks white, and even then never alone. Is that understood?'

The boys nodded.

'Good. Now I'm freezing to death out

here and I expect Lady Collins is, too, so I think we will go back into the nice warm house.'

'Uncle James, can we go and see the puppies?' David asked.

'Yes, but don't run, and come in when you get cold,' James said, knowing they would probably pay no attention to his directions once they were out of sight.

Emma put Helen down so she could go with the others, before walking with James.

'Was the short lecture the voice of experience?' she asked.

'Guilty as charged. My brother and I sneaked out on to the ice one day when it was much too thin. The price of our impatience was that we fell through. Fortunately it was a shallow part of the lake so we were able to clamber out on our own. We were soaked through and frozen to the bone, but we found it to be very educational, especially when our father heard about it.'

'I imagine you miss your brother.'

'Yes, I do, and my wife, too. Thank

goodness I still have the girls and Katherine as well. I don't see Katherine and her family all that often, but we do write fairly frequently. Family is important,' James said as they entered the house.

* * *

An early luncheon was over and Emma was dressed in her travelling cloak, bonnet, gloves and half boots at the top of the front steps.

Her carriage had arrived yesterday, as expected, and was now standing at the bottom of the steps. In the cold air the horses' breath looked like steam. Her baggage was in the boot, Molly was inside, the grooms were huddled into thick overcoats as they sat on the box and a footman stood ready to open the door.

'Lady Benfield,' Emma said, 'thank you so much for looking after me. It has been a real pleasure.'

'The pleasure has been all mine, and if you come through Baldock on your way back north, please do come and stay. I shall be delighted to see you.'

'Lord and Lady Weston, I am glad to have made your acquaintance,' Emma said, exchanging courtesies with them.

Emma crouched down to embrace Sarah and Helen who both hugged her back. She kissed them both on their foreheads.

'Thank you for all the lovely stories,' Sarah said.

'I wish you could stay,' Helen said and a tear rolled down her cheek.

Emma wiped away the tear.

'I have to go and see my brother and his family, before they think I have got lost or run away to sea. We will see each other when you go to London. Your papa has said he will take us all one day to see the show which has lots of horses. We must look forward to that.'

The girls nodded and Emma straightened up to face James who was standing behind his daughters.

'I too will look forward to our visit to Astley's,' James said, as he reached for her hand. He kissed her fingers. 'Until then.'

Emma smiled tremulously before turning and hurrying down to her carriage.

As the carriage rolled down the drive, the frozen gravel crunching under the wheels, she looked back and waved to the family who were waving back from the steps.

The family all went inside and James turned slowly to follow them, accompanied by his mother.

'You should ask her to marry you,' she said quietly.

'What did you say?' James stopped and turned to face his mother.

'You should ask her to marry you,' she repeated. 'I think you suit very well.'

'I can't do that! Nobody wants to marry a cripple like me unless they want his title or his money and I don't think she cares about either.

'Besides, you said yourself she has no plans to remarry. Then, even if she did decide to remarry, she could take her pick of the eligible bachelors and could certainly do far better than me.'

'She doesn't seem bothered by your

injury and, as you say, already has a title. However, I do think she might like some security and two daughters that she already holds in affection. I think she already holds you in affection, too, and, if I'm not mistaken, it's mutual.'

James stared at his mother as he considered what she had said.

'And,' she continued with a raised eyebrow, 'just because she has no plans to marry at the moment, doesn't mean that she has no intention of ever marrying again. She could change her mind.

'Who knows what she might say if the right person was asking her?' She wagged an admonishing finger at him. 'Furthermore, you undervalue yourself and finally, you protest too much.'

The dowager took one last long look at her son before turning and entering the house. James followed even more slowly than usual.

Half in Love

Emma felt hollow as her carriage headed for the Great North Road and thence to Mayfair.

It had only been a few days with the Benfield family, but she had enjoyed herself a great deal. They were warm and sociable, far more than Peter's family had ever been. The Collinses were friendly but always a little reserved, a little distant, as if she was suffered rather than welcomed.

It was part of the reason she was reluctant to move to the dower house in Spalding. She suspected she might find herself set apart from Peter's cousin and his family and end up very solitary as a consequence.

Emma sighed and Molly glanced at her speculatively before resuming her survey of the shops as they passed through the centre of Baldock.

Emma wished she had daughters like Sarah and Helen who were quite adorable. Their father was charming, too.

She had now seen what she wanted but didn't have. She would have to give serious consideration to getting married again.

She was still young and it wasn't too late to start her own family, but nor could she wait for too long. She didn't need a grand passion or another youthful Peter. Someone kind and affectionate would do.

Perhaps her brother Lionel might know some suitable gentlemen, or could introduce her to London society where she might meet someone appropriate.

It was a pity James was still in love with his dead wife and so set against remarriage, she was already more than half in love with him and he would have been perfect.

They arrived in Stratton Street just as the light was beginning to fade. The carriage pulled up in front of a tall red brick house.

As Emma stepped down, the front door opened and a footman hurried down the house steps to assist her.

Then, just as she entered the front door, her brother emerged from his study at the back.

'Emma! At last! We had expected you a couple of days ago, then we didn't understand from your letter exactly what happened.'

'It was too complicated for a letter when I was about to see you in a day or so. Sit me in front of a tea tray and I shall explain.'

They kissed cheeks and Emma handed her gloves, hat and coat to the butler.

'Certainly, come upstairs to the drawing-room. Ophelia went shopping but she should be back at any moment.'

By the time Emma had a restorative cup of tea in front of her, her sister-in-law Ophelia had joined them, so Emma only had to tell the tale once.

'That was very civil of them,' Ophelia said. 'You say Earl Benfield and family are coming to stay with Baron Weston?' She turned to her husband. 'Do we know the Westons?'

'I know of him, as inevitably our paths

cross in the House of Lords, but not very well, as he sits on the other side of the chamber.

'I haven't met Benfield. I suppose his politics may be the same as Weston's, but quite possibly he stays in Rutland most of the year.'

'Regardless of their political affiliation, we should invite them all to dinner, since they have been so kind to Emma. Perhaps next week.' She turned back to Emma.

'The day after tomorrow we have a few friends coming to dine. We should like you to meet the Reverend Basil Goodman. You really should marry again and he's eminently suitable.

'He's not much older than you and already a rector in Kensington. Lionel knows his bishop uncle very well from the House of Lords and Basil will undoubtedly become a bishop too before very long.'

'I shall be delighted to meet him,' Emma said in a faint voice. She had forgotten how forceful and managing her sister-in-law could be.

Yes, she had more or less decided she should marry again, but hadn't expected to have eligible men pushed in front of her quite so soon. Perhaps Ophelia didn't really want Emma living in her house, and this was a clue as to how things would be?

Not a Good Start

James was pleased to be spending time with the rest of his family, but now Emma had gone to London, he had a constant feeling something, or rather, someone, was missing. It didn't take him much introspection to understand why he felt that way.

His mother's remarks kept coming back to him, although he knew the idea of marrying Emma was hopeless and preposterous because she had no intention of getting married again.

Nevertheless, he had business to attend to in London and, as well, a promise to keep at Astley's, didn't he? So, he urged Victor and family not to dally in Baldock, after all, they would soon be back there for the Christmas holidays, wouldn't they?

Emma felt as if she had barely settled in at Stratton Street when the dinner party was upon them.

As the guests arrived they were shown into the drawing-room and Emma was introduced to them as they arrived. Two gentlemen entered the room, both wearing dog collars — clearly the bishop and the rector.

They were an odd pair, one being short, portly and older, and therefore surely the bishop. The other was tall, thin, probably in his late twenties.

'Emma, my dear,' Ophelia said, 'may I introduce his Grace the Bishop of Chertsey and his nephew the Reverend Goodman. Gentlemen, my sister-in-law, Lady Collins.'

They bowed and Emma curtseyed. As she looked up she saw that the bishop was looking her up and down, before looking back to Ophelia.

'Your Grace, I wonder if I might have a word with you,' Ophelia said, before walking away with the bishop.

So, Emma thought, it didn't take Ophelia long to throw me at the rector. She looked up at him. He was very tall, already had receding hair and his dog collar was a loose fit around a scrawny neck.

He reminded her of a tortoise sticking its head out of its shell. He swallowed and his prominent Adam's apple bobbed up and down. He didn't look very promising so far, but perhaps his personality made up for it.

'I understand you are a rector in Kensington, reverend,' she said.

'Yes, indeed. Prince Augustus Frederick is one of my parishioners, although of course he has his own chaplain.'

He smiled and Emma was a little taken aback to see he had protruding front teeth as well. Good lord, she thought, a tortoise with teeth like a squirrel and the first thing he tells me is how he is acquainted with the royal family.

Ophelia cannot be serious, she thought, here was I hoping for someone like James, but this person is not even remotely comparable. The only way he could be superior to James is in a footrace.

Emma resolved to be polite, but careful not to encourage the reverend. Later she would have to have a frank discussion with Ophelia.

The opportunity to speak with Ophelia did not arise until the following morning. After breakfast, and Lionel had gone about his business, Emma followed Ophelia to the morning-room. Emma got straight to the point.

'Ophelia, how did you ever imagine I would wish to marry the Reverend Goodman?'

Ophelia looked surprised.

'But he has excellent prospects and you're not in a position to pick and choose, are you?'

For a few moments Emma was lost for words and simply gaped at Ophelia.

'What do you mean 'not in a position to pick and choose'?'

'You're not exactly a débutante with a large dowry or even a rich widow with her own establishment, are you?'

'I have a perfectly adequate portion and a dower house to go with it. I'm not obliged to marry at all if I don't choose to.'

Ophelia sniffed.

'I suppose if you wish to vanish into

the wilds of Lincolnshire and become a recluse, you can, but I cannot imagine anyone preferring that to moving around in London society.

'Plus, the rector is very well connected and marriage to him would also be a great help to Lionel in his political career. You've been married once before on your own terms and now I think you should take a wider view and consider the rest of the family. You're not going to get any younger, are you? Dwindling away in the wilds of Lincolnshire is no good to anybody.'

Emma took a deep breath. Obviously she and Ophelia viewed the situation quite differently. Quarrelling was not going to help.

'Perhaps Baron Weston or Lionel might introduce me to someone else whom I find more suitable.'

'Perhaps they will. I sent dinner invitations to the Westons and Benfields yesterday.'

'The Benfields?' Emma had noticed that Ophelia referred to the Benfields in the plural.

'Yes, it was the Earl and Countess Benfield that you stayed with in Baldock, wasn't it?'

'Yes, but the Countess Benfield is still in Baldock as far as I know and not likely to come for dinner.'

'But I thought you said the earl was bringing his daughters to present at court. Why would he not come with his wife?'

Emma burst out laughing. Her sister-in-law was so wrapped up in her own affairs and plans that she obviously hadn't been listening. As Emma laughed, Ophelia started to look thunderous.

'He didn't bring his wife because he is a widower. Countess Benfield is the dowager countess. His wife is presumably in a churchyard somewhere in Oakham. His daughters are only six and eight years old, so a little too young to be presented and it's not the season anyway.

'The earl is coming to London because he has business to attend to in the City. He combined the trip with a

Christmas visit to his mother and sister, so he could hardly leave his daughters behind, could he?'

'What? Why did nobody tell me all this?'

'I did, but you must not have been paying attention. You can see for yourself when he calls, as he will probably bring his daughters with him. He has promised to take them and me to Astley's Amphitheatre and said he will invite your boys, too, if they are interested.'

Ophelia looked very cross and suddenly stood.

'There has been a misunderstanding. I need to speak to Lionel.'

Oh dear, Emma thought, sobering quickly. This is not at all a good start if I am to live in this house. Even if it could be arranged for me to have a separate apartment, I don't think Ophelia wants me here. In any case, I am a guest and must try to be more conciliatory.

Her introspection was interrupted by the butler who offered her a note on his tray.

'The messenger is waiting to see if there is a reply my lady.'

Emma opened the note.

'Would it be convenient to visit Astley's Amphitheatre tomorrow afternoon? If so, I will call for you, and possibly your nephews as well, at two o'clock. Benfield.'

Perfect. This escape was just what Emma needed. After that prosy bore the Reverend Goodman and the friction with Ophelia, it would be good to spend time with the Benfields and away from Stratton Street.

She wasn't sure if she could last until the New Year in the same house as Ophelia.

'Please tell the messenger that it will be very convenient, thank you.'

'Very good, my lady,' the butler said and went off to pass on the message.

Emma couldn't help comparing the two men. The reverend was perfectly awful and James? James was quite wonderful. She was definitely more than half in love with him, but it would never do, because she knew he didn't plan to marry again. If only she could find someone just like him.

In the meantime, she would make the most of their time together tomorrow as friends and when he came to dinner. On the way home to Spalding she would call on Lady Benfield and possibly he might still be there, but otherwise they wouldn't see each other again. Life would never seem quite the same again after that chance meeting in Sawtry.

Made for Each Other

'My Lady, two carriages have drawn up outside,' the butler said to Emma and Lionel
where they were waiting in the reception
room. Emma was already dressed and ready
to go, anticipating that James would be on
time. She knew they would need to be at
Astley's a little early for the performance in
order to give James time to make his slow
way inside. Lionel was in the reception
room with her to see what kind of man was
this Earl Benfield.

'Two?' Emma asked and she went to
the window to look out. 'Oh, I think the
second one is Baron Weston. They must
have decided to come as well.'

Emma and her brother went to the
front door just as it was opened for Victor. Lionel's three sons materialised in
excited anticipation behind their father.

'Lord Weston, are you coming too?'
Emma asked.

'Oh yes. As soon as Robert and David
got wind of the outing, they demanded

to come as well. Consequently Katherine and I had to come with them. James offers his apologies for not descending from the carriage so as not to waste a lot of time.'

He glanced at Lionel and Emma took the hint.

'Lord Weston, may I introduce my brother, Viscount Finch.' The two men shook hands. 'Lionel, this is Baron Weston and if you will follow me down to the carriage, I will introduce you to Earl Benfield.'

Lionel looked puzzled, clearly wondering why Benfield was staying in the carriage and not coming to the door as would be conventional.

'Lord Benfield was injured in the war and has difficulty walking,' Emma explained briefly as she followed Victor down the steps. Lionel mouthed a silent 'Oh' of understanding and went with her.

As she left the doorway, Emma saw two happy looking girls with their faces pressed to the windows of the carriage. She smiled, gave them a little wave and they grinned and waved back.

James's valet, Norton, was with them

to help James move about and he opened the door as Emma approached.

'Good afternoon, Lady Collins,' James said, extending his hand.

Rather than shaking his hand, as he may have intended, Emma used it to steady herself and entered the carriage to sit next to him.

'Good afternoon, my lord, may I introduce my brother, Viscount Finch?'

Lionel reached in and shook James's hand.

'Benfield. I shall look forward to speaking with you when you come for dinner. In the meantime, thank you for taking my boys with you as time is hanging heavy on their hands during the school holidays.'

'Not at all, Finch, I think the children enjoy it more when there is a group of them. I have two nephews in the other carriage as well. Now, if you boys climb in here and sit with your backs to the horses, the girls can squeeze in with us.'

Emma looked at Sarah and patted the seat between herself and James. Sarah moved across and then Emma picked up Helen to sit on her lap. Helen looked up at Emma and seemed very pleased with herself. Sarah watched the boys closely as they scrambled in to sit facing them.

Lionel closed the door behind them with a click and went to greet the occupants of the other carriage.

'Let me introduce my nephews, who are Luke, Andrew and Matthew,' Emma said, pointing to them one by one. 'Boys, this is Lord Benfield and his daughters Sarah and Helen.'

'Hello, sir,' the boys chorused, while the carriage rocked a little as Norton climbed up to the box.

'Are you boys interested in horses?' James asked.

'Oh, yes sir,' Luke answered, who appeared to be the eldest, 'but there's not much opportunity for riding now we're either at school or spending a lot of time in town.'

'We have ponies at home in Oakham,' Sarah volunteered, 'and papa teaches us because he used to be a Captain of Hussars.'

'Oh, famous!' Andrew said in an excited and breathy voice. 'Will you tell us all about the Hussars, sir?'

All the boys were clearly awed at the prospect of travelling to an equestrian show with a Captain of Hussars. Sarah looked very proud of her father and put her hand in the crook of his elbow. Helen just cuddled closer in to Emma.

'I was in the Fifteenth Light Dragoons until I was injured. Sergeant-Major Astley, who created today's show, was also in the Fifteenth Light Dragoons, but well before my time, so we've never met.

'Unfortunately, now I have difficulty standing without walking sticks, I am no longer able to ride a horse standing on its bare back,' James said with a straight face.

The boy's jaws fell open and they stared at James with eyes like saucers.

'No doubt you will see how it is done this afternoon,' James said, 'but you must not try it yourselves until you are much older, otherwise we shall all be in trouble with your parents.'

The boys looked at each other. Emma cast an enquiring glance at James who winked at her.

On their return from the show, the boys were even more animated and simply babbling with excitement. As they drew up outside the house in Stratton Street, Emma reminded them to thank their host before they raced inside to tell their father all about it.

Emma kissed the girls on their foreheads, and they then moved across to the other seat.

'Thank you, James, for a wonderful afternoon,' Emma said and very nearly kissed him too before she remembered herself. Their eyes locked and they squeezed hands.

'I'll call on you tomorrow,' James said.

'No. You will stay at home,' Emma said in a voice which clearly brooked no argument, 'you've had a very tiring day. I shall call on you instead.' He nodded agreement and she smiled briefly before stepping down on to the pavement.

She entered the house and climbed up to the drawing-room, still with a little smile on her face. Emma there discovered her nephews bombarding a bemused father with tales of the acts they had seen.

Andrew stood with his legs apart and hands waving in the air, as he described the man carrying flags whilst riding bareback on two horses. Then Luke demonstrated how a chariot had been driven around the ring by galloping around the room holding imaginary reins.

Not to be outdone, Matthew starting telling him what the clown had done while Emma crossed to the bell and rang for tea.

Once the boys had gone to their rooms to play equestrian games, and Emma had restored herself with a vital cup of tea, Lionel looked his sister in the eye.

'Did you enjoy the outing?' he asked.

'Oh, yes, enormously, and all the children had great fun.'

'And Lord Benfield?'

'I did wonder if it might remind him of

what he had lost, but he seemed to enjoy it, too. He was even explaining some of the finer points of the horsemanship to me.'

Lionel regarded her thoughtfully.

'What exactly is your relationship? Is he courting you?'

Emma sighed and shook her head.

'No, we're just friends. He has said he doesn't plan to remarry.'

'Do you wish he was courting you?'

There was a longer pause as Emma considered the question being posed by her perceptive brother. She pressed her lips together before nodding.

'Ah.'

'Yes, I think I fell in love with him at his mother's house in Baldock.'

'Why does he not want to remarry? Do you know?'

'His mother said he is very conscious of his injury. Excessively so, in her opinion. I think it silly, too, and a case of misplaced pride. In any case, if my feelings are not reciprocated, it would be foolish to let it go any further.

'No, I think after Christmas I should go back to Spalding and move to the dower house. I've considered it all and I can afford to run a governess cart and pony which will be quite sufficient to get around the neighbourhood.'

'I hear you were not impressed by the Reverend Goodman?'

Emma shuddered.

'No. He's dreadfully pompous and full of self-importance. If he makes any morning visits you have my permission to send him away.'

'Don't be surprised if Ophelia parades more men in front of you. She is firmly of the opinion that you should remarry.'

'Yes, I know, and I'm not against the idea in principle, but I would need to be convinced I was doing the right thing.' Emma kept to herself her opinion of why Ophelia wanted her to marry again.

Playing Cupid

The next day, mid-morning, Emma walked around to Half Moon Street with Molly trailing behind her. It had seemed pointless to get a carriage out for what was only a ten-minute walk and while it was cold, it wasn't raining. No sooner had Emma surrendered her hat, coat and gloves than Katherine appeared.

'Lady Collins, how good of you to call,' Katherine said. 'Tell me, may I call you Emma and hope that you will call me Katherine? I meant to ask you in Baldock. I do hope we can be friends if you are going to be living in London now.'

'Yes, please do call me Emma, but I'm not at all sure I shall be living here. At the moment I think it more likely I shall go back to Spalding to live.'

'Oh,' Katherine said with a slight frown, 'I had hoped we would see more of you.'

They entered the drawing-room to find a maid putting a tray of tea things on a table. James and Victor were sitting next to each other and chatting. As the ladies entered, Victor sprang to his feet and came to greet Emma, who noticed James about to struggle to his feet as well.

'No, James, don't get up,' Emma said, using his Christian name without thinking.

Katherine looked at her husband with a slightly raised eyebrow.

'Good morning, Lord Weston,' Emma said with a nod. Emma then went over to James, smiled and clasped his hand, before taking the chair vacated by Victor.

'Emma, do you plan to visit the theatre while you are here?' Katherine asked.

'I hadn't thought about it, but it would be a pity to waste the opportunity, as theatre in Spalding is infrequent and there is little to praise in it. Is there anything you suggest?'

'Unfortunately the excellent Mrs Siddons has just retired. I hear there is a new actor, a Mr Edmund Kean, who is very promising and due to make his debut next month. In the meantime I have been recommended 'The Hollow Tree' and 'Cupid and The Giant' at the Sans Pareil Theatre.'

'Do you plan to go? I would be interested, but I have nobody to go with me and I can't possibly go on my own.'

Katherine couldn't help smirking. Emma had said exactly the right thing, as if she had read the same script and knew when to give Katherine her cue.

'I think Victor and I will be busy for the next few evenings,' Katherine said, staring meaningfully at her husband. She turned to James with a broad smile. 'But I know James has made no mention of invitations, so he must surely be free and able to take you.'

James looked startled by his sister's ambush and took a moment to recover.

'Oh now, Katherine, I'm sure you said nothing about being busy every evening this week and it would be a struggle for me to get into a theatre. Besides, we don't have our own box and there may not be another free at short notice.'

Katherine had no intention of letting

James wriggle out of escorting Emma to the theatre. She was entirely convinced it would do them both good. Katherine agreed with her mother that James and Emma were surely made for each other, even if they couldn't see it themselves.

Seeing their behaviour together at Astley's the day before, any casual observer would be forgiven for thinking they were already married. Katherine wasn't going to lose any opportunity for pushing them towards each other.

'I'm sure Victor can find a box, can't you?' Katherine said, looking at him with a steely eye.

Victor shrugged helplessly and nodded.

Emma tried hard not to grin at Katherine's brazen manipulation which, in any case, suited her perfectly.

'If we take your valet to assist you and my maid for propriety, I'm sure we will manage,' Emma said, sealing James's fate. She did so want to visit the theatre and she did so want to spend an evening alone with James as well. Alone, that is, apart from her maid and his valet.

The door opened and Sarah came in followed by Helen, Robert and David.

'Lady Collins!' Sarah cried and both girls hurried over to take one of Emma's hands each.

'If you will excuse me,' Victor said, heading for the door, 'I shall go and see about finding a box at the theatre.'

'Theatre?' Robert said. 'Is there a pantomime?'

The adults all looked at each other.

'I'll find out,' Victor said with a wry smile.

Emma stayed for lunch, and soon afterwards the news came back that there was indeed a box available that evening at the Sans Pareil and a pantomime at the same theatre every afternoon, except Sunday, for the next few weeks.

'Emma, may I have the pleasure of your company at the theatre this evening?' James asked, acknowledging the inevitable. 'As you suggested, we can take my valet and your maid. No doubt they will be happy to sit at the back of the box and watch the performance, too.'

'Thank you, James, I shall be delighted,' Emma said, who really was delighted. Katherine looked very smug.

★ ★ ★

The Sans Pareil was on the Strand. It was a fairly new theatre and quite small. James's carriage arrived at the theatre very early, well before the crowds arrived, which was just as well, since it was in any case a busy street.

The front of the theatre had four Grecian columns at the front and between the middle two were double doors leading to the expensive seats, while single doors to either side led to the cheap seats.

As James's carriage drew up, two uniformed porters threw the double doors wide and then blocked the pavement so that James's aristocratic progress into the theatre was not impeded by random pedestrians.

An usher led the way to their box. James's progress was slow and he leaned on his valet's shoulder. Emma and her maid followed behind them as the stairs and passageway up to the box were narrow.

'Well,' James said, standing at the entrance to the box, 'this is a bit smaller than the usual, isn't it?'

'Shall I go first?' Emma asked. 'Then I can steady you as you take your seat.'

'Perhaps that is wise. It wouldn't do for me to stumble and go flying over the edge, would it?'

Emma was conscious of James's pride and how he might not want his slow and halting progress to be on public display.

'I certainly hope not, you might take me with you. At least the theatre is empty now, so there is nobody to see us if we make fools of ourselves.' Emma took the seat nearest the stage with James beside her. Norton and Molly took the two seats at the back of the box.

'I see,' Emma said, reading the programme, 'the first play is by a Miss Jane Scott. It is unusual to find a female playwright, isn't it?'

'What is it about?'

'It is described as a 'Grand Eastern melodramatic Burletta'. Something about the tyranny of the Brahmins and females being sacrificed to their gods. Frankly it sounds inordinately complicated to me.'

'Never mind, I expect it will be colourful and with some exotic dancing. I doubt we will have to focus too closely on the dialogue. What about the second one?'

''The Fairy of the Fountain' or 'Cupid and the Giant', is a ballet rather than a play, some sort of love story told in dance.'

'A giant ballet dancer should be interesting,' James said.

At the end of the second part, Emma sat back and looked at James.

'What did you think of it?' he asked.

'The dancing in the last part was fine although I was disappointed not to see the giant ballet dancer. To be honest, I thought the story in the play was a bit tenuous and the acting satisfactory rather than outstanding.'

James's face fell.

'But I enjoyed it tremendously,' Emma continued.

James looked confused.

'Sometimes it's not what you do that matters, but who you do it with.'

She grasped his hand as they looked at each other thoughtfully. Emma then realised that taking his hand was perhaps inappropriate and rather forward of her. She went to pull it away, but James's hand tightened on hers so that she couldn't. He glanced over the rail at the crowd below who were making their way out.

'I see they have the latest modern arrangement down below. The pit has been pushed back behind a fence and there is seating right in front of the stage. I suspect that is the best place from which to see the pantomime. How many of us will there be?'

Emma thought for a moment.

'Assuming all the children and their parents go, that is twelve. Then the girls' nursemaid, your valet and myself — that makes fifteen.' She turned to Molly sitting behind her. 'Would you like to go?'

Molly was surprised and glanced quickly at James's valet. Emma was fairly sure that Norton gave her a tiny nod.

'Yes, if you please, my lady.'

'Then there are sixteen of us,' Emma said.

'Norton, while we wait for the crowd to clear, go down to the box office and tell them we want sixteen seats for the day after tomorrow. I think in the middle of the first two rows would be best.'

He turned back to Emma.

'If the children sit in the first row, the adults can sit just behind them and we should all have a good view.'

They watched the audience filing out while they waited for Norton to return. The smartly dressed people in the front rows were leaving quietly through doors near the stage. Those behind the fence were talking loudly and laughing as they pushed towards the doors at the back. Norton returned.

'I'm sorry sir, but the ticket office says

most of the seats are already sold for Saturday. They ask if the Monday afternoon performance would suit you.'

James looked at Emma, who shrugged. She didn't mind what day it was as long as she had the right company.

'Yes, tell them Monday will be fine.'

To the Rescue

The following morning, an annoyed Emma was sitting in the morning-room with three gentleman visitors. Ostensibly they had called upon Ophelia, but no sooner had the third gentleman arrived than Ophelia found an excuse to leave the room. Since Molly had been put in a corner as a chaperone, there was little that Emma could do about it without being uncivil.

The first to arrive had been the Reverend Goodman. Emma didn't know if Lionel hadn't told Ophelia that the reverend could be sent packing or Ophelia had simply ignored the information. Either way, the rector didn't improve on a second meeting.

Paradoxically Emma was somewhat relieved when a second gentleman, Mr Patterson, arrived. She hoped that she might be able deflect one with the other, but the men seemed to have little in common. It became a barely disguised competition between them to impress Emma.

On the one hand Emma didn't care how many royal patrons the reverend had or hoped to have. On the other hand she didn't care either that Mr Patterson was wealthy, was buying a large estate in darkest Oxfordshire and hoped to find a lady capable of running his new house.

The two of them went quiet when a third gentleman was announced and they looked keenly at the door to see if it was another potential rival for Emma's hand.

It seemed that Sir Albert Potter was a prominent member of the House of Commons and another connection of Lionel. Emma could only suppose that Sir Albert was hoping to gain some political advantage by marrying Lionel's sister.

He appeared to be nearly twice Emma's age and she could not imagine why Ophelia thought she might be interested in an ageing politician. Perhaps Ophelia was having difficulty in finding candidates, since the social season had ended and parliament was closed until the New Year.

Emma's initial irritation had increased to annoyance. Now she had three gentlemen trying to score points off one other. Did they suppose that she was obliged to marry? Did they think she would be gratefully choosing whichever man was best and whom would be condescending enough to make her an offer?

As none of them was making much effort to engage her attention, she was free to wonder what Ophelia had said to them and how much longer the mantel clock would tick before they would take themselves off.

'Earl Benfield,' the butler intoned, and Emma breathed a sigh of relief. Rescue was at hand. She sprang to her feet and the men necessarily followed suit.

They looked at the new arrival moving slowly into the room on his walking sticks. Reverend Goodman probably wondered how well he was connected. Mr Patterson probably wondered how much he was worth. Sir Albert probably wondered what his political affiliation was, if any.

As James came forward to be introduced, they all relaxed, as this decrepit fellow was clearly no threat to their aspirations.

When the other visitors had arrived, Emma had carefully selected an individual chair for herself so as to not get too close to any one of them. Now she guided James to the sofa and then sat beside him.

'Lord Benfield,' Sir Albert said, 'I have not seen you around the Houses of Parliament. Have you not taken your seat?'

'I have, but quite some time ago, and I rarely come to London,' James answered.

'No, I see that could be difficult for you. I suppose you had an accident?' a rather tactless Sir Albert continued.

'You might call it an accident. My horse fell on my legs and broke several bones which were never set properly.'

'Most regrettable,' Mr Patterson said in a very patronising voice. 'Once I move to my new estate I intend engaging a first-class stable master to train my horses and teach me to ride competently as well.'

'I'm sure that is an excellent idea, Mr Anderson,' James said drily.

'Patterson.'

James waved his hand dismissively, making it clear he really didn't care what the man's name was.

'I trust you sacked your stable master and had the horse shot?' the reverend asked.

James studied him with narrowed eyes for a long moment.

'It was not necessary, vicar, for the French had already shot my horse.'

'Rector,' the Reverend Goodman corrected into the sudden silence.

'I do beg your pardon, Rector Woodman,' James said.

'The French?' Sir Albert asked, looking puzzled.

'At the time I was in Spain, fighting the French as a Captain of Hussars,' James said, looking at Sir Albert with hard eyes.

The mantel clock ticked loudly as some careless assumptions were rapidly revised. This was not some penniless invalid minor earl normally stuck in the country and of no consequence. This was an earl with money and who could afford to be a Hussar, which was not a cheap regiment.

Not only that, but he was a hero of the war against the French. He obviously had no involvement in politics as he didn't bother to come to the House of Lords very often.

Then he was sufficiently sure enough of himself to show he didn't care who they were, either, since he deliberately forgot their names. Finally, it was clear that Lady Collins favoured him as she had sat next to him on the sofa.

It was time to cut their losses and so they all suddenly noticed the time and recalled other appointments.

Once the door had closed on the last of her unwanted visitors, Emma turned to James.

'Thank you, James, for my rescue, I

can see now how the Hussars rout the French. You were very intimidating to those gentlemen.'

'Self-important fools, the whole lot of them . . . '

Before James could continue, the door opened again and Ophelia entered in a rush. She stopped in confusion and looked around, obviously expecting to see the other three men and not expecting to see James. Molly was still sitting in the corner.

James took a walking stick and went to rise, but Emma put her hand on his forearm and pushed him back down.

'Ophelia, may I introduce Earl Benfield? You must excuse him from not rising, as it is painful for him to do so.'

Emma knew she was overstating the case somewhat, but didn't care.

'Oh,' Ophelia said, 'you must excuse me, I wasn't informed that you were here, I was expecting someone else.'

'Lord Benfield, may I introduce my sister-in-law Lady Finch?'

They shook hands.

'My lord, I'm pleased to meet you, Emma has told us how you were good enough to assist her at the inn.'

'It was the least I could do after Lady Collins was kind enough to comfort and reassure my two small frightened daughters during the fire.'

'Did they catch the horse thieves?'

'I don't know. I doubt it, somehow. I imagine they are now stabled at some less reputable staging inn a long way from Sawtry. I shall stop and ask at the inn on my way home to Oakham but I don't expect there to be any news.'

'Will you be staying in London over Christmas and the New Year?'

'No, we will be going back to my mother's house in Baldock for Christmas. My sister, Lady Weston, and her family will then return here, but I shall go directly back to Oakham.'

Emma knew the time would come when she would have to say goodbye to James and the girls, but she had been trying not to think about it. Now the depressing reality was forced upon her.

'When do you expect to leave for Baldock?' Emma asked.

'In about ten days. In the meantime, thank you for your dinner invitation, Lady Finch, we are looking forward to it.

'However, now it is time I was leaving, as I have business to attend to this afternoon if I am to get everything done before I go home. Would you be so kind as to call my valet to assist me? He should be waiting in the entrance hall.'

As Ophelia went off to call Norton, James pushed himself to his feet with his walking sticks. Emma took his arm to steady him.

'James, we shall see you tomorrow at the pantomime. Is everybody going?'

'Absolutely. The boys are relating the events of last year's pantomime to the girls, who are getting very excited at the prospect. We were still in mourning for my wife and my brother a year ago and so the girls didn't go to the panto of that year nor of the previous year. Anything before that was too long ago for them to remember.'

Emma squeezed his arm gently as Norton arrived to help his master to the carriage. As Emma was reflecting on the late earl and late countess and the effect on the others, Ophelia came back into the room.

'I hope you're not throwing your cap at Earl Benfield,' she said.

'What do you mean?'

'It would be a waste of mine and everybody else's time. I understand he doesn't intend to remarry and besides, he's crippled.'

'He's a fine gentleman and a kind friend,' Emma said, not liking Ophelia's tone or description. 'Why should we not be friends? What does it matter if he was disabled in the service of his country?'

'It matters if you ever want to have a family of your own. If he's that badly injured, it's probably not just his legs which don't work properly any more. If you want children you would do better to consider the other gentlemen who came this afternoon and cosying up to the earl is likely to discourage them.'

Emma was stunned by Ophelia's remarks and just stared at her back as she swept from the room.

A Night at the Theatre

On Monday afternoon, four carriages arrived in front of the Sans Pareil Theatre to disgorge seven excited children, six doting adults and three busy servants. Amy and Mollie ushered the children inside to the front row of seats while the others followed. James and his valet brought up the rear.

The Finches and Westons sat in the second row on the left side of the aisle, while Emma and Molly went into the right hand side, leaving the two seats nearest the aisle for James and Norton. Sarah and Helen sat in front of James and Emma, with Amy at the end in front of Molly.

'Lady Collins,' Sarah said, turning around, 'what story are we going to see?'

'It's called 'Aladdin and the Wonderful Lamp'.'

'What's it about?'

'You'll have to listen carefully to the story, but it's about a boy called Aladdin who has a wicked uncle called Abanazar.'

'Are you sure?' Robert, who was sitting next to Sarah, asked. 'I thought the wicked uncle was called James!'

'Impertinent boy!' James said in mock anger. 'Your uncle James is a kind and generous man. Just for saying he is wicked, I shall have you strapped to the roof of the coach on the way home, even if it is snowing by then.'

Robert laughed and faced the front again.

Sarah looked, with wide eyes and an open mouth, between her cousin Robert who was being impertinent and her father who was enjoying a joke with him. Her attention switched back to Emma.

'What does the wicked uncle do to be wicked?'

'He's not really Aladdin's uncle but needs a boy to go into a cave and get a magic lamp for him, then he leaves Aladdin in the cave, which is not very nice, is it?'

'No. Does he get out?'

'Oh yes, he gets out and marries the

princess.'

'There's a princess too?' Sarah put both her hands over her mouth in excitement.

'Is she pretty, the princess?' Helen asked. She had been listening to the exchange intently.

'Oh, I'm sure she will be and I expect Aladdin is handsome too,' Emma said, 'but you'll see for yourselves very soon.'

'But I expect the wicked uncle Abanazar is very ugly,' James said, pulling a face at them as grotesque as he could manage.

The girls burst out laughing and faced the front again.

'It seems to me,' Emma said to James, 'you are still a boy at heart and you are going to enjoy this as much as the children. I wonder that you don't take to the stage.'

'Oh, I would,' he said, 'but there is always a chase scene and, frankly, I would be terrible at that, wouldn't I?'

She looked at him with a wry smile and patted his arm. It was a mercy, she thought, that he could joke about his disability rather than get depressed about it.

By then the theatre was starting to fill and everybody was looking around at everybody else. A happy buzz rose from the crowd, assisted by the excited chattering of the children in the front row. Before long, a man dressed in colourful flowing robes and a turban stepped out from the middle of the stage curtains and raised his arms. An expectant hush gradually fell over the audience.

'My lords, ladies, gentlemen — and mischievous children,' he cried and gave a maniacal grin at the children in the front row. 'This is the story of the poor boy Aladdin who lives with his mother in a laundry in China.

'Then one day a visitor arrives . . . '

He swept his arm towards the stage and walked to the side as the curtains opened.

The children quickly learned to boo and hiss when the wicked uncle Abanazar arrived on the stage and cheer when Aladdin appeared. There were cries of 'He's behind you!' when Aladdin seemed not to notice how Abanazar was stealing up behind him.

They were all impressed when the genie appeared with a flash and crack of pyrotechnics from the lamp. Then there were the traditional arguments of 'Oh yes, he is' and 'Oh no, he isn't' between actors and audience and finally at the end, three curtain calls.

Only when Emma went to clap the actors at the end did she realise that James had been holding her hand all the time, under cover of all the excitement in the theatre. As everybody applauded, she and James exchanged small smiles. Anybody observing them, Emma thought, might assume they were simply pleased by the performance.

They let the rest of the audience leave before them, so James's slow progress wouldn't hold everybody up. As they were waiting, Luke clapped his hands and intoned in the deepest voice he could manage, 'Master, I am your servant to command.' Then Andrew would tell him 'Oh no, you're not!' to which Matthew would reply 'Oh yes, he is!' and a heated exchange would continue for several minutes. As they filed out, Sarah and Helen took Emma's hands while they followed James, who was supported by Norton.

Their carriages were waiting for them as they left the theatre. In the slight chaos of getting the children in the right coaches, James took Emma's hand and raised it to his lips.

'Don't you dare call on me, I shall call on you tomorrow,' Emma said firmly, to which James nodded, before Norton assisted him into the carriage. Emma turned to Sarah and Helen who were waiting with Amy.

'Did you two enjoy it?' Emma asked.

'Oh yes, Lady Collins, we had a wonderful time,' Sarah said and Helen nodded enthusiastically.

Amy helped the girls into the carriage with James while Emma moved to her own carriage with Molly. Emma was looking forward, with pleased anticipation, of calling on James tomorrow.

Marriage in Mind

As Emma entered Weston House the next day, she could hear James playing the piano in the music room.

The butler conducted her upstairs and silently opened the door. As he did so, the music swelled in volume and several female heads looked her way.

She hesitated in the doorway, as she had not expected to find a crowd of ladies. Katherine hurried across and drew Emma back out of the room, closing the door behind her.

'Emma, how lovely to see you,' Katherine said in a quiet voice. 'Come along to my sitting-room. James will no doubt be playing for some time yet and that will keep our other visitors occupied while we have a chat.'

They went a short distance down the hall before entering a small sitting-room. Katherine left the door ajar so they could still hear the music or any more arrivals.

'So what did you think of the panto

yesterday?' Katherine asked after they were seated comfortably.

'I thought it was very well done. My nephews are still talking of it today.'

'Yes, and the children here were so animated by it they took ages to settle down in bed. Once they did settle, they suddenly went to sleep, I think they must have been worn out. If they had had sore throats from all the shouting I wouldn't have been surprised,' Katherine said.

'It's a pleasure to see children enjoying themselves so much. They didn't seem too keen on coming to London when we were in Sawtry.'

'Very true, and you seemed to enjoy it as well. I wasn't sure if we would see you today or not in case you needed a rest, too.'

'I shouldn't say it,' Emma said, 'but I am escaping my sister-in-law, as well as calling on James as I promised. Yesterday morning Ophelia sprang some gentleman visitors on me and I'm afraid she'll do it again today. I was rescued by James, who did a good job of making them uncomfortable, so they took themselves off.'

'Oh? I don't understand. He didn't say anything about it. You have to explain a little more.'

'The other gentlemen visitors tried to patronise the poor invalid who was badly injured because the fellow couldn't manage to stay on a horse.

'James then played the Captain of Hussars card, so they were very embarrassed when they realised they had got it so completely wrong. As soon as they decently could, they left.'

'Good for James, but why were the men there?'

Emma huffed with annoyance as she recalled being caught by surprise yesterday.

'It seems clear that my sister-in-law doesn't want another lady living in her house. I wouldn't interfere with the household, but perhaps she doesn't want to take the chance of me influencing my brother in a way that doesn't suit her.

'Consequently she is throwing eligible

gentlemen at me, hoping one of them will take my fancy.

'She also admits she would like to create a little political advantage for her husband, too, but I resent being used as a pawn for her benefit. So far I will be happy to not see any of her selected suitors again.'

'I had thought you were not planning to remarry?'

'I wasn't, but I've concluded I should consider the possibility. However, I think it most likely that I shall return to Spalding and set myself up with a small household in the dower house.'

'I had thought . . . ' Katherine's eyes strayed towards the open door. She gave her head a little shake. 'I have to say, in my own defence, that our lady visitors this morning are none of my doing. I'm definitely not springing ladies on James.'

'They were not expected?'

'No, absolutely not. Besides, he's been quite emphatic he won't marry again. Clearly some of the ladies haven't considered this might be the case, otherwise they wouldn't have bothered dragging their unmarried daughters along.'

'Are there many? I couldn't see from the doorway.'

'Three ladies and four daughters between them. If any more arrive, the music room will be getting crowded. I don't know how they knew he was here and they have clearly come to see him, not me, never mind their excuses. I barely know any of them.'

'Somebody would have seen his crest on the doors of his carriage. The news will have spread like wildfire below stairs and in the mews too, as there's so little to gossip about at this time of year.'

'I suppose so. He was practising when they arrived and he hasn't stopped. I think it's to avoid making small talk with them.'

Emma and Katherine sat quietly for a few minutes listening to the music.

'He can't play for ever, can he?'

Katherine said. 'We shall soon have to go back in there.'

'Now I suppose it's my turn to rescue

him, isn't it?' Emma said, wondering how she could do so.

As soon as they could hear the piece of music was clearly coming to an end, they stood and sauntered back to the music room. A final flourish died away and they went in as the small audience was applauding.

James ignored the audience and was very busy sorting through the sheet music, while Katherine introduced Emma to Lady Horley and her daughter the Honourable Hortense Horley.

Emma wondered what Lady Horley had been thinking of when they named the daughter Hortense. Presumably Hortense herself was hoping to marry a titled gentleman, and probably any titled gentleman, provided their name did not begin with the letter H and thus rid herself of her alliterative burden. Earl Benfield would do nicely, for example.

Next Emma was introduced to Mrs Mortenson. Mrs Mortenson was built along the same lines as a shire horse, as was her daughter. They both had heavy features and broad hips. Certainly the poor unfortunate girl was a very considerable distance from being described as a diamond of the first water.

Emma tried not to wince when her hand was gripped tightly by Mrs Mortenson in a handshake.

Emma speculated that Mrs Mortenson might think that a handicapped earl with no sons, would find a strong girl with big hips and good child-bearing potential an acceptable proposition, even if the girl was stout and had coarse features. Mrs Mortenson probably thought his choices were limited.

Finally Emma was introduced to Lady Thurston who was as slim as Mrs Mortenson was broad. Her two daughters were equally slim, dainty, very pretty and very young.

Emma wondered if James would be enticed by girls barely half his age. She couldn't image either of them coping with two stepdaughters only ten years younger than themselves.

Lady Thurston looked carefully at

Emma, who was obviously much closer in age to James and a very attractive lady, too. Her eyes flicked to Emma's left hand. Emma still wore her wedding ring and Lady Thurston's face relaxed into a polite smile.

'We have not met before, I think?' she said.

'No, I live near Spalding in Lincoln-shire. I am only visiting London to spend Christmas with my brother, Viscount Finch.'

'Oh, I see. And is Lord Collins with you?'

'No, he is still in Lincolnshire.' Emma knew, as she said it, she was being decep-tive, even if it was the literal truth.

She debated whether or not to explain how the present Baron Collins was not her husband. She quickly decided not to clarify the matter, as she didn't care for the current conversation, which was tak-ing on the tone of an interrogation. Let Lady Thurston think what she liked.

Emma moved on to James, who was still seated at the piano.

'James, your playing is excellent as usual, I never tire of hearing it,' Emma said in a clear and carrying voice. She smiled at him warmly and offered her hand which he raised to his lips, not being slow on the uptake.

'Emma, my dear,' he replied, also in a carrying voice, 'it is always a pleasure to play for you, you should have come earlier.'

'No matter, I shall be sure to come earlier next time. In the meantime I'm sure your visitors have enjoyed the music.' She looked at the other ladies as she said it, allowing James to retain hold of her hand.

She saw the other ladies were rapidly drawing their own, incorrect, conclusions about her relationship with James.

They were all rising to their feet, ready to remove their daughters from an improper situation, where the earl had an adulterous relationship with a married lady. There was clearly no morally acceptable scope for their daughters to become Countess Benfield.

Emma drew up a chair so she could sit next to James, while Katherine ushered her visitors out.

'If I am not mistaken,' James said softly, 'you have just routed some encroaching mothers and their innocent lambs.'

'You could hardly wait for the cavalry to arrive, could you? Considering you are the cavalry. Besides, I am returning the favour of yesterday.'

Emma felt little pang of sadness as she was reminded how she would be returning to Spalding after Christmas while he would be going back to Oakham. Then there would be no reason for her path to cross with that of this dear man.

'What would you like me to play for you?' he asked.

'Oh, I don't know,' she said with a sigh, 'something cheerful.'

He lifted an eyebrow in enquiry.

Emma thought quickly.

'The weather is so cold and grey, we need something bright.'

Katherine returned to the room and hesitated as she saw them sitting together.

'Katherine,' Emma said, before she could leave the room, 'do you think we could call the children and sing a few carols?'

'Certainly. Why not? I shall go and find them.' Katherine left Emma and James alone as she went to find the children.

'So, James, were you not attracted to the Honourable Hortense Horley?'

'Good heavens, no! If the parents had so little sense as to name their daughter like that, it doesn't auger well for the girl to have any sense, either, does it?'

'What about the Thurston girls?'

'Those schoolgirls? I'm probably old enough to be their father. It would be like adopting an elder sister for Sarah and Helen. No, it's ridiculous.

'Lady Thurston is dreaming if she thinks I would have any interest in them. Anyway, you did a fine job of convincing them that you are my adulterous mistress, so I doubt we shall see them again.' James frowned. 'I'm not happy you may have destroyed your reputation in the process.'

'Oh, pah!' Emma waved away his concerns. 'We can let it be known in due course that I am a widow and in any case I will be back in Spalding before long.

Nobody there will care about or believe a rumour like that.'

Her explanation didn't make James's frown disappear from his forehead.

'There is always the Mortenson girl. She looks strong and well able to bear many sons,' Emma said.

James barked with laughter.

'She might be, and I'm sorry for her, but . . . ' James was saved from further comment by the opening of the door and the entrance of two girls and two boys.

Sarah and Helen ran over and Emma crouched down to hug them both.

'Are you going to sing some carols with us?' she asked.

'Yes, please,' Sarah said, 'but I'm not sure if we'll know the words.'

'Don't worry about that, you join in if you know the words, and if you don't you can just hum or listen and enjoy them anyway. Shall we sit together on the sofa?'

They went over to a sofa where Emma

sat in the middle and put an arm around each girl. Katherine and the boys went and sat on the facing sofa.

James looked over the top of the piano at the very domestic scene. On one side was his sister and her children. On the other side . . . Could they be his family? He loved his daughters to distraction and . . . he loved Emma too. She obviously had affection for Sarah and Helen. James thought she held him in affection as well. She certainly wasn't averse to him.

She didn't seem bothered by his disability, either, although she did make sensible allowances for it. Was she determined to remain single and move back to Spalding or would she consider another possibility?

James resolved to ask her if she would marry him. The idea that she might laugh at the idea or say it was absurd, was daunting, but if he didn't ask, he was sure he would always regret it.

She certainly might say no, but he was sure she would say it kindly and not mock him. However, this was not the time or place. Although, perhaps it might be best if he sounded her out first, to avoid embarrassment for her and humiliation for him.

More Haste . . .

The carols came to an end and Katherine ushered the children away. It was time for Emma to depart as well. James put a hand on Emma's arm to delay her for a moment.

'So tell me, you know how you had a variety of gentlemen in your company yesterday . . . are you positively inclined towards any of them?' he asked, providing her with an opportunity to give him a hint.

'Oh no, I wouldn't consider marrying any of them,' Emma said with a laugh.

She moved to the door as Katherine arrived to conduct her back downstairs.

Oh well, thought James, sagging a little on the piano stool, that's an end of it. She isn't prepared to entertain marriage to any of us.

Emma collected Molly on her way out and was glad that she had elected to come by carriage.

The day was still freezing and icy, so

walking was not an attractive prospect.

They were soon back in Stratton Street and Emma hurried from the carriage to get back into the warm as soon as possible. However, it would have been wiser to wait for a footman to help her down.

As it was, it was a large step down on to the icy pavement where her foot slipped and Emma went flying. She landed heavily on her side and her head banged hard on the first step of the house. Molly's cry of alarm alerted the footman on duty at the front door.

Very quickly Emma was surrounded by a concerned coachman, footman and butler as well as Molly. The cook's face appeared from the area steps to see what was happening.

'Ooh, Molly give me your hand,' Emma said as she tried to stand up, wincing as she put her weight on one of her feet.

The footman grabbed her arm as she teetered and looked as if she was about to fall again.

'John,' the butler said, 'carry her ladyship up to her room. Gently now!'

'Edward,' he then said to a second footman who had emerged to see what was going on, 'run and call the doctor, but be careful you don't slip as well. And John, when you come back down, you can tell me why there wasn't more salt and sand on this pavement.'

Once a shaken Emma was in her room, Molly carefully removed Emma's boot and stockings to reveal an ankle which was already starting to swell. Emma's head was still ringing from where it had hit the step and tears trickled down her cheeks from the pain.

Molly hurried down to the kitchens for ice to put around the ankle. At least there was no difficulty in getting ice at this time of year. The doctor came promptly and after some gentle examination, gave as his opinion that nothing was broken.

However, she was to stay off her feet for several days which would also give the bruising on her face and hip time to subside. He gave her a few drops of laudanum in a glass of water and told her to sleep a little if she could.

Once the doctor had gone, Ophelia came to see her.

'Emma, I'm so sorry. The butler says he offers his apologies and the footman has been reprimanded for not seeing that more salt was put down both on the steps and on the pavement too, to clear the ice.'

'Don't be too hard on him. It was partly my fault for being in a hurry to get into the warm. I should have waited for someone to help me down and steady me on the slippery ground.'

Ophelia took Emma's hand.

'No, you mustn't blame yourself. It's bitterly cold out there today and the servants should have been more attentive. I shall make sure the maids keep a good fire in here and now you must try to sleep as the doctor said. I will send a note around to the Westons to cancel the dinner party. You obviously can't come downstairs just yet and without you it would be a bit pointless.'

Emma bit her lip in disappointment and a tear squeezed from her eye. She had been looking forward to the dinner and she had ruined it all.

'I see you are in pain,' Ophelia said. 'The doctor said he had given you some laudanum and you really must try to sleep a little.'

Emma nodded, but the movement made the bruise on her face hurt, so she pressed Ophelia's hand before letting it go.

* * *

'James,' Katherine said, 'I've just had a short note from Lady Finch. She says she regrets, but she has to cancel the dinner, due to illness.'

'Illness? Does she say what illness or who is ill?'

'No, it doesn't say. It's just a short note and I have the impression it was written hurriedly.'

Ah well, James thought, in this case the illness was likely to be a fabrication and just an excuse. It was not even a postponement of the dinner, but a cancellation.

Emma was giving him a message earlier, now he considered it. Hindsight was a wonderfully clear way of seeing things.

She had been hinting that he should be considering marriage to some girl even if she had chased away the particular ones which were there. Then, secondly, she was very emphatic that she wouldn't marry any of her visitors yesterday, including him.

Singing carols with all of us, was because she wouldn't see us again before Christmas, nor afterwards either. It was a way of saying goodbye to Sarah and Helen without actually saying goodbye.

She was tactful, because they were sure to be upset when they realised they wouldn't see their new friend any more. He was going to be upset, too. She must have realised he was on the point of offering her marriage and decided to avoid it without anyone getting embarrassed.

Asking her sister-in-law to cancel the dinner was a convenient way of cutting the connection. Illness didn't normally strike so suddenly.

'Emma was well when she left here,' Katherine said. 'Do you suppose she will call again tomorrow? No doubt she will tell us then who is unwell.'

'Perhaps, but I'm definitely not expecting her,' James said. In fact he wasn't expecting to see her ever again and consequently he really wanted to be on his own for a while.

He swallowed and took a deep breath before he could choke with disappointment.

'If you will excuse me, I shall go up to my room, as I have some letters to write.'

Lost Love

Emma was sitting up in bed, drinking her morning cup of tea, preferring it to the chocolate popular with many ladies.

She had slept, thanks to the laudanum, but she hadn't slept well. Her aches and pains hurt every time she moved, so now she felt worn out, but not sleepy.

Staying in bed was not a difficult instruction to follow, and as she wasn't getting up, she had sent Molly back downstairs with instructions to bring up breakfast on a tray in 20 minutes.

Emma lay in her bed, having little to do but think. She could hear people moving around in the house and the occasional clip-clop of a horse passing in the street below her window.

Molly had opened the curtains, but the daylight was very watery.

Emma supposed it was yet another grey, cold, winter's day and she was glad to stay in the warm — not that there was much choice in the matter.

She wondered what James had thought when he heard about her accident.

She wished he would call, but was sure he wouldn't. It was not the weather for somebody using walking sticks to venture abroad.

Even if he called, he couldn't come up to her bedroom and she couldn't go downstairs, so it would be entirely pointless for him to come in the first place.

It would be nice if he sent her flowers and a note, she thought. Then she banished the thought.

There were no flowers to be had on a cold winter's day like this, unless one had a hothouse, which the Weston's didn't.

She would be happy though, to get a letter from him. If he couldn't get flowers, perhaps he would send her a novel to read while she was stuck in bed.

Molly appeared with her breakfast, which distracted Emma from her daydreaming. She was hungry, having missed out on her dinner last night.

★ ★ ★

James had also slept badly. His sleep was full of bad dreams where Emma was always just out of reach and walking away. He couldn't reach her because he couldn't walk properly and he was too slow to catch up with her.

Consequently, he woke up in a very bad mood. He lay in bed wondering what to do with himself today.

Time, he thought, to send Miss Trellis her dismissal, a flattering reference and three months' salary.

She should be more than satisfied, he thought, and then, thank goodness, he need not see her stiff and uncaring face again.

However, Sarah and Helen still needed a governess, especially if there was now no prospect of a stepmother.

Amy was all well and good for feeding and clothing them, but hadn't the wit to teach them anything.

He would write a note for a footman to take to the employment agency.

James was in no mood to venture out in this weather, especially if the ground was frosty. The agency could come to him with details of suitable governesses.

Norton helped him dress and get downstairs to Victor's study where he wrote the short note asking the agency to call.

Indeed, Mrs Trump came from the Agency for Superior Butlers, Governesses and Other Staff within the hour.

Business was probably very slow just before Christmas.

James received her in Victor's study. She was plump, had dyed yellow hair which could well have been a wig, and a worried frown on her face.

'Good morning, Mrs Trump,' James said. 'Forgive me for not standing. You may recall from our last meeting that it is difficult for me. Please take a seat.'

'Good morning, my lord. I'm sorry if Miss Trellis has left your employ, but I must remind you that our fees are refunded only if the employee is found to be unsatisfactory in the first month.'

James waved dismissively.

'This is not an issue, Mrs Trump. The case is more one of . . . Miss Trellis not being a good match for my household.'

Mrs Trump's frown disappeared to be replaced by narrowed eyes. She was obviously wondering if James had made improper advances and been repulsed.

'I have given her an excellent reference and no doubt she will be in contact with you in due course.

'I am in need of a replacement who can either join us here immediately or shortly after Christmas at my mother's house in Baldock.

'However, this time I wish to interview at least three candidates and also for them to meet my daughters. It is important that my daughters get along with their governess and vice versa.'

Mrs Trump's face cleared. The problem with Miss Trellis was evident.

'Do you have any special requirements this time, my lord?'

James pursed his lips as he considered the question.

'They need to be amiable and have some imagination. Proficiency in subjects such as Italian or music are of little importance at this stage.

'It would be an advantage if they were familiar with the countryside and even better if they can ride or drive. City girls might be a bit lost at Oakham.'

'Very good, sir, I shall check the files, but I'm sure I can find some that might suit. When should I send them to see you?'

'I think, Mrs Trump, I should like you to bring them tomorrow.'

She was a little startled and her eyes widened as she rapidly evaluated who might be available at short notice.

'Bring them? And tomorrow, my lord?'

'Yes, I want to have the matter resolved as quickly as possible. Tomorrow after-noon, perhaps two o'clock, will be most convenient.'

'Very well, my lord, I shall do my best.' She rose, curtseyed and hurried to the door as James rang the bell for a foot-man to show her out.

James rubbed his face. He must speak to Katherine and make sure she didn't go off somewhere with Sarah and Helen tomorrow and also to Victor to make sure he could use his study tomorrow afternoon, too.

Let us hope, he thought, Mrs Trump presents us with someone more enthusiastic than the dour Miss Trellis.

★ ★ ★

Late that morning, after the doctor had called once more, Ophelia went to see Emma.

'How do you feel now, Emma?' Ophelia asked. 'Has the pain eased a little?'

'I'm still bruised, battered, foolish and full of aches and pains,' Emma said, as she was feeling very sorry for herself.

'Oh no, don't say that, it really wasn't your fault. The servants should have cleared the ice and been quicker to help you down to the ground as well.

'They are perfectly capable of looking out of the window to see what the weather is like.

'As well, they knew you would be returning shortly and should have been on the lookout for you.'

'No, no, it was mostly my fault. I wasn't thinking clearly and I was too hasty. Now you've had to cancel the dinner, too.'

'Never mind that, they'll understand. When you are up and about, we'll renew the invitation.'

But it will be too late, a miserable Emma thought, they'll have gone to Baldock, then Oakham, and I won't see James ever again.

'Is there anything I can do for you?' Ophelia asked.

Yes, Emma said to herself, you can beg James to come and keep me company. Emma knew this was utterly impossible for many reasons, not least of which was Ophelia's disapproval of him.

'Yes, you could find me a book to read, please, while I am stuck here,' was all Emma could actually say to her sister-in-law.

Ophelia returned shortly afterwards with a Gothic novel that Emma thanked her for warmly.

However, the book was dark and gloomy and did absolutely nothing to raise her spirits.

In mid-afternoon Ophelia came back.

'Rector Goodman has called to see you. I said you were indisposed and unable to go down.

'He asked me to convey his best wishes for a quick recovery. Do you have any message for him before he leaves?'

Emma was still in pain and thus not in the best of moods. She stared at Ophelia in amazement and it was a minute or so before she could find a reply.

'I wonder how and why he is a clergyman if he is so insensitive to other people.'

'Whatever can you mean?'

'I mean he can go away and not come back, I have no wish to see him now or in the future.

'I thought he had understood this before. You can tell him it again and perhaps he will understand this time.'

Ophelia frowned her annoyance.

'I can see your discomforts have put you entirely out of countenance. I shall thank him for his concern and send him on his way.' Ophelia huffed and left the bedroom.

Emma wondered who was being persistent, the rector or Ophelia. She turned on her side and winced. She turned on to her other side.

The only person she wanted to see was James and she hadn't heard anything from him at all.

She loved him and thought he cared for her, too. Obviously not, when she was injured and he simply ignored her.

Surely if he cared for her even only a very tiny little bit, he would have enquired after her or sent a sympathetic note.

Emma felt very alone, despite being surrounded by people. Tears fell from her eyes and she dabbed them dry with the edge of the linen sheet.

Should she go home to Spalding just after Christmas or wait until the New Year?

She might as well go home as soon as there was a break in the weather, and start her move to the dower house. There was nothing for her now in London and no point in delaying the move.

A Kind Heart

James called his daughters to come and see him after they had all breakfasted.

'I have written to Miss Trellis and said she is not to go home with us to Oakham.'

Both girls looked at him with surprise and questions in their eyes.

'Some other governesses are going to come and see us this afternoon and we will see if we can choose a new one. This time I want both of you to meet them, and them to meet you, before we decide which one suits us best.'

'Papa, does that mean we can choose the one we like most?' Sarah asked.

'It has to be one that I think will be a good governess, but yes, it also has to be one you like as well.'

'What if we don't like any of them?'

'Well,' James said, hesitating and seeing a potential problem ahead, 'then we shall have to ask to see some more of them until we find one we do like.'

Sarah looked thoughtful. Helen looked

a little worried. Robert appeared in the doorway.

'Are you coming upstairs to play?' he asked.

Sarah looked a question at her father and James nodded and waved them away.

After lunch, the butler came into the reception room.

'My lord, there is a Mrs Trump with three ladies to see you.'

'Very good, send just Mrs Trump in to see me, please,' James said, who was sitting on a sofa with Sarah and Helen either side of him, having anticipated Mrs Trump would be on time.

'Papa, is Mrs Trump a governess?' Sarah asked.

'No, she is a lady who is helping me find a governess for you. I am expecting her to have brought three governesses with her for us to meet.'

The door opened again.

'Mrs Trump, my lord.'

Mrs Trump came in and curtseyed, taking a look at Sarah and Helen as she did so.

'Thank you for bringing us some candidates, please take a seat.' James waved her to a seat facing them.

'Thank you, my lord, I have three ladies for you to interview, but please realise they may not be ideal. However, they were all I had available at such short notice. If none of them suits you, I can find others, given a little more time.

'Today I have brought Miss Felicity Brocklethorpe. She is rather young and would be unsuitable for a household with older boys, but she has been educated at the very best establishments.

'Then I have Miss Verity Crampton who comes highly recommended and has an impeccable background. Her father is a vicar in the Cotswolds.

'Finally there is Miss Mary Williams. Her previous employer was a diplomat who has been posted to Spain and has taken his family with him. Miss Williams chose to remain in this country.'

'Very good, Mrs Trump, that is all understood. Before you send them in, please explain if you will, that I have difficulty standing, and that it means no disrespect if I don't rise when they come in. Now if you would send in the first one, please.'

'Thank you, I shall send in Miss Brocklethorpe.'

A few moments later, Miss Brocklethorpe came in and James's eyebrows rose. She was young, slim but curvaceous, blue-eyed and had a riot of golden curls around her face. James understood immediately why she would not suit a household with older boys. He wasn't convinced she would suit his household, either, if he wanted the footmen to concentrate on their duties.

'Good afternoon, Miss Brocklethorpe, please take a seat. Have you been a governess long?'

'Oh no, sir,' she said shyly, 'this is the first time, but Father said that it was time I made use of an expensive education and moved amongst the nobility.'

'I see,' James said, a little taken aback by this forthright information. 'Who is your father?'

'He is a coal and wine importer in Wapping. We have a house overlooking the river and Father has lots of ships.'

'Ah, yes. I understand now,' James said, as he understood very well. Her father was obviously wealthy and wanted his daughter to move up in the world.

Since he had no entry amongst the gentry or aristocracy, sending his daughter to be a governess was a way to get her through the door.

A pretty girl with a wealthy father should be able to find herself a titled but impoverished husband. Her plain speaking in this case would probably work even better than learning to be more tactful.

However, the titled but penniless husband wasn't him for any number of reasons and she wasn't a sensible choice of governess for the girls, either.

'Thank you for coming, Miss Brocklethorpe. We live in an isolated part of the countryside which is unlikely to suit someone used to city life such as yourself. Please ask Mrs Trump to send in the next lady.'

She curtseyed and James looked at Sarah and Helen.

As the door clicked shut, Sarah pulled a face which said she was not impressed.

'She has hair like my doll Jemima, doesn't she, Papa?' Helen piped up.

'Yes, Helen, she does, exactly the same. Let us see what the next one is like, shall we?'

The door opened again and a tall lady walked in and curtseyed. She wore a plain brown, rather shapeless dress and her hair was pulled back tightly in a severe bun.

'Miss Crampton?'

'Yes, my lord.'

'Please take a seat and tell us a little about yourself.'

Miss Crampton sat straight and rigidly in the chair.

'My father is a vicar and I have been brought up with a firm understanding of discipline and proper behaviour. My last post was in Richmond with a large family.

'The older boys began to misbehave and their father was not prepared to correct them, so I felt obliged to resign.'

James noticed from the corner of his

eye that Sarah was looking up at him. He glanced down and saw that she looked worried.

'Is this a good Christian family, sir?' Miss Crampton asked.

'Why yes, we attend church nearly every Sunday.'

'And do you assemble the staff for prayers each morning?'

'No, not since my grandfather's day, but I imagine the staff say prayers on their own in the morning or evening and they are certainly free to do so.'

'If you will excuse me sir, I think I would not suit your household.' So saying, she rose, gave a perfunctory curtsey and left the room.

James was a bit taken aback. He was not used to being the one dismissed. He glanced down at the girls. Sarah was blowing her cheeks out with relief. Helen looked up at him anxiously.

'Papa, can we not have Lady Collins as our governess?'

'No, Helen, I'm afraid not. Lady Collins is not a governess and she will surely be going back to her own house after Christmas.'

Helen pouted in annoyance.

The next candidate entered the room. She was much older than the other two, perhaps in her mid-thirties or early forties, with a pleasant face.

She also wore a fairly plain brown dress but at least this one fitted her. She had her hair in a bun, too, but it wasn't nearly as tight and severe as the way Miss Crampton wore hers.

'Miss Williams, please take a seat and tell us about yourself.'

'Thank you, my lord. I was governess to three children at a house in Kent. Their father has taken up a diplomatic post in Madrid where I understand it can be fiercely hot in summer and bitterly cold in winter.

'Also they would be living in the centre of the city which I did not think I would enjoy, as I have always lived in the countryside, so I chose to stay in England. Are these two girls all of your children, sir?'

'Yes, this one is Lady Sarah,' he said, pointing to his left, 'and this one,' pointing to his right, 'is Lady Helen.'

'How do you do,' Miss Williams said, with a slight bow of acknowledgement. 'What subject do you girls like most of all?'

'I like reading best,' Sarah volunteered.

'And I like drawing best,' Helen added, 'but not of sheep.'

'Oh. I see. I like reading, too. There's nothing better than a good story, is there? Why don't you like drawing sheep, Lady Helen?'

'Because they're boring. Besides, they're just white blobs and how can you draw a white blob?'

'Yes, I do see what you mean. It would be rather easier to draw the sheepdog, wouldn't it? Never mind, there are lots of other things to draw like flowers and trees, aren't there?'

Helen nodded vigorously. Miss Williams smiled warmly at them both.

'Do you like dogs, Miss Williams?' Sarah asked.

195

'Oh, yes. I had a dog when I was a girl, but governesses can't really have a dog of their own, it wouldn't be suitable for them.'

James was convinced. This one was warm and friendly and clearly interested in the girls. It was time to get the opinion of Sarah and Helen.

'Miss Williams, if I were to offer you the post, when would you be available?'

'Immediately, sir. My previous family have already left. They are spending Christmas with relations in Hampshire and then will sail to Spain from Portsmouth, so I am already free.'

'Thank you, Miss Williams. Would you return to Mrs Trump and then ask her to return to me?'

As soon as the door clicked shut behind her, James turned to his daughters.

'Well, what did you think of this one?'

'I think she was nice. I like her,' Helen said.

'I liked her, too, but Papa, when we get home can we have a dog, please?' Sarah asked.

James sighed in resignation.

'A dog? I suppose so. There are dogs on the home farm, we can see if one of them would do.'

'No, no, a pet dog puppy, Papa, not a farm dog,' Sarah said very firmly. 'I want one to be with me to cuddle, not one that chases sheep.'

'A pet dog and one that is a puppy. Very well, but you'll have to look after it yourself. We might have to wait a while as well, until there is a puppy old enough to leave its mother, since you don't want one already trained to herd sheep.'

'Thank you, Papa,' Sarah said, leaning her head against James's arm.

Mrs Trump came back into the room.

'Did one of them suit you, sir?'

'Yes, we think Miss Williams will do nicely. Please ask her to come back, then you can depart with the others. Send the bill for your fee here to me rather than my man of business.'

'Thank you, my lord, it is my pleasure to assist you.' Mrs Trump curtseyed and left the room. A few moments later a footman opened the door for Miss Williams to come back in.

'Miss Williams, I would like to offer you the post. You will be paid ten pounds per month, full board, a clothing allowance and have one day off per week. In Oakham you will have your own sitting-room and be jointly responsible with Lady Sarah and Lady Helen for the care and training of a pet dog which we will acquire in due course. Is that acceptable?'

'Yes, thank you, sir, very acceptable. Do you wish me to start at once?'

'Yes, it will be most convenient if you do. Just a moment.' He rang the bell and the butler appeared.

'This is Miss Williams, the new governess,' James said. 'Tell a footman to go with her in a cab to her lodgings to fetch her things and then ask the housekeeper to make up a suitable room. Thank you, Miss Williams, we will see you shortly.'

She followed the butler from the room.

'And you two girls may go and find Aunt Katherine to tell her about your new governess and how we will be getting a pet dog, too.'

The girls kissed him on the cheek and scampered off to find their aunt.

James was left to mull things over. Sometimes you don't fully appreciate what you have lost until it is gone. He had fallen in love with Emma and wished she would marry him. But she had made it quite clear that she wasn't going to marry again and had hinted him away to avoid embarrassment.

He had hoped that she loved him in return, but clearly the affection she had for him was the affection of a friend. A friend who was caring enough to suggest he should marry someone else.

But he didn't want to marry one of those young girls, he wanted to marry Emma, a beautiful woman with a kind heart who didn't seem to mind his difficulty walking. A woman who didn't need his home, his title or his money but cared for him as a man and a friend.

She seemed to like his daughters, too, but at least there he hoped Miss Williams might be a good replacement for Miss Trellis. He didn't know why he hadn't replaced Miss Trellis before. Perhaps she hadn't been visible enough for him to notice.

James could see he was going to become lonely. He had made an effort not to think too much about his wife after the initial grief and just concentrate on getting on with life.

Now he had been knocked out of his self-imposed shell and had to face what he was missing. If Sarah and Helen were getting a dog, perhaps he should get one too, so at least he had some sort of company on the long quiet evenings.

His reveries were interrupted by his sister Katherine.

'I hear you have hired a replacement for Miss Trellis.'

'Yes, I should have done it ages ago. I don't think Miss Trellis is cut out to be a governess but she probably had no choice. There's not much alternative for an unmarried lady with no money and I suspect she hated it.'

'Sarah and Helen were full of enthusiasm for the new one and they say they're getting a puppy, too.'

'Yes, I hope I don't regret either decision. Miss Williams has gone to get her things and you can meet her when she gets back.'

'Have you heard any more from the Finches or Lady Collins?'

'No, but I wasn't really expecting to.'

Katherine looked at her brother who appeared unusually glum. She had thought James and Emma were going to make a match of it, but it didn't seem to be happening. If James wasn't going to see Emma and Emma wasn't coming to see James, had they fallen out with each other?

Katherine certainly hadn't noticed anything amiss. They had apparently been on very good terms the last time Emma had left here to go home. Had there been a discreet exchange of letters?

Was the 'illness' really a sham and a polite excuse to avoid an awkward dinner? She didn't know what was going on, but whatever it was, Katherine decided she had to get to the bottom of it.

She loved her brother and liked Emma a great deal and would like nothing better if they married. There was no reason why she should not visit her friend, was there?

'I think I shall call on them tomorrow and see what the illness is. If it is something infectious I shall only leave a card, I wouldn't want to pass it on to the children.'

James nodded but didn't make any further comment.

In Want of a Wife

'What did the doctor say today?' Ophelia asked Emma.

'He said I may get out of bed and sit in a chair, but I am not to move about or go downstairs until he has seen me again. Frankly, this bruise on my face looks hideous and I have no desire to show it to everyone anyway.' Emma had told a reluctant Molly to give her a hand-held looking-glass and then been horrified by the huge dark patch on her face.

'Don't worry, the bruises will soon fade. How are your wrist and ankle?'

'Painful, but he assures me they should be much improved by tomorrow . . .' Emma was interrupted by a light knocking on the bedroom door. Ophelia went to see who it was.

'Excuse me, my lady,' the butler said, standing in the hallway, 'there is a Lady Weston below enquiring for Lady Collins. What shall I say?'

'You may tell her that we are not

receiving today,' Ophelia said.

'No, wait!' Emma called from her bed. 'Please ask her to wait, I would like to see her. Send a chambermaid up to assist Molly while I get out of bed.'

'Very good, my lady,' the butler said and walked off down the corridor with his usual stately tread.

Ophelia spluttered helplessly, looking between the disappearing butler and Emma.

'But Emma, you can't entertain visitors. You're not supposed to go downstairs and you can't ask a visitor to come to your bed chamber.'

'Oh, nonsense, Katherine is a friend, not just any visitor, and she will think nothing of it. Would you be so kind as to give her tea while I get up? It will inevitably take me a little longer than usual.'

Ophelia shook her head, shrugged a little and left the room. Moments later, a chambermaid came in to see why she was needed and Molly emerged from the dressing-room.

'Good,' Emma said, 'the two of you

can help me out of bed and steady me while I get dressed. Molly, something simple if you please, and never mind about stockings as they won't fit over the bandage anyway.'

Twenty minutes later, Emma was sitting in a chair getting her breath back after dressing rather awkwardly and painfully. The chambermaid had gone to fetch a second chair. Molly had gone downstairs to invite Lady Weston up to the bedchamber.

Katherine entered the bedroom a little cautiously as Ophelia had not been very forthcoming about Emma's illness. She saw Emma sitting in a chair with a huge purple bruise on the side of her face and Katherine's eyes widened in surprise.

'Oh, my dear! My goodness, Emma, what happened to you?' Katherine said, hurrying across to Emma, hands outstretched. Emma reached out to take Katherine's hands and Katherine then hesitated as she saw the bandage on Emma's wrist.

'I was totally stupid,' Emma said. 'I was in a hurry to get into the warm after returning from your house and slipped on the icy pavement. I went flying, twisted my ankle and wrist, bruised my hip and smacked my face on the step.' She gestured vaguely at her face.

Katherine winced in sympathy.

'It must be very painful, but you didn't break anything?'

'No, thank goodness, and it should all pass in a few days. My bruised dignity will eventually recover, too.'

'I'm so sorry to hear all this but at least you don't have any dreadful disease.'

'Disease?'

'Your sister-in-law sent a note that said someone was ill without giving any details, so we all thought the worst. We were worried there might be disease in the house, and I had to come and find out.'

Emma thought this over. Why had Ophelia been so vague? Was she trying distance them from the Westons? And was this why James hadn't called? Even so, it was a little unfeeling of him to not even send a note.

She was reluctant to ask Katherine why

James was ignoring her, as her feelings would be all too obvious and it would be embarrassing. She was also a little afraid of what she might hear in return.

'Oh no, no disease, except clumsiness, that is. How are your family, Katherine? No accidents on the icy ground, I hope. This cold weather seems very severe this year.'

'No, they're fine, although James is in poor spirits. Perhaps he is missing your company?' Katherine asked, raising an eyebrow.

Emma didn't know what to say. She clearly couldn't visit at the moment and also couldn't think of what she could add without sounding pathetic.

'The girls are in high spirits,' Katherine added. 'They have a new governess and have been promised a pet dog before long.'

'A new governess?'

'Yes, a Miss Williams, James appointed her yesterday and she moved in immediately. The girls like her immensely, at least so far, which is encouraging.'

'What is she like?' Emma asked, hoping to hear that she was old, fat and ugly.

'She's about thirty-five years old I should guess, very motherly and brought up in the countryside, so Oakham should suit her.'

Emma had to know.

'Plump? Pretty? Tall?'

Katherine looked carefully at Emma as she considered the question.

'About the same height as me, handsome rather than pretty, slim, pleasant-looking, a dog lover apparently, hence James's agreement for the girls to get a puppy.'

Emma swallowed. She wasn't jealous. Definitely not. She was stuck here and this Miss Williams was there, looking after Sarah, Helen and maybe James too. Miss Williams was probably much more attractive than Katherine had wanted to admit. Life was hard sometimes. That was just how it was.

'Will you be going to Baldock soon?'

'Yes, next week. James has, I think, finished his business, the House of Lords has closed until next year and the weather is much too cold for the children to go out sightseeing, even if Miss Williams is there now to take them.

'The weather doesn't look very promising, and we should go before it gets even worse and makes travelling difficult.'

'Oh, I agree. Hopefully by the time Christmas is over, my bruises will have healed and the weather improved because it's a long way to Spalding.'

'I'm sorry to find you so knocked about, but relieved that you don't have some dreadful disease,' Katherine said. 'I'm sure James and the others will be glad to hear it too.'

'Give them my regards,' Emma said, 'and perhaps I shall see you before you go to your mother's house?'

'I'm sure you will,' Katherine said. She stood, clasped Emma's uninjured hand and kissed her unbruised cheek. Molly sprang to her feet from the stool in the corner and opened the door for her. Katherine smiled and waggled her fingers at Emma before following Molly downstairs.

Emma was pleased to have had a visit from her friend, but still wondered why she had heard nothing from James. Even if Ophelia had made them think there was a disease in the house, he could have sent a note.

Katherine hadn't said anything, but had Ophelia somehow given the impression Emma and the irritating Rector Goodman had some sort of understanding? Why was Ophelia still promoting the rector anyway? And had the handsome Miss Williams made James forget all about the rather plain widowed Lady Collins already? Emma wiped away a tear.

★ ★ ★

As soon as Katherine reached home, she went looking for James. She found him gloomily attending to some correspondence in Victor's study.

'James, I've just been to see Emma and the poor dear has had an accident.'

'An accident? What sort of accident?' James sat up straight, his full attention on his sister and his heart starting to race. 'Is she badly hurt?'

'She was in too much of a hurry to get home, slipped on the icy pavement and fell awkwardly. She is full of bruises, has a twisted ankle, a sprained wrist, and is feeling completely sorry for herself. I suspect she is feeling neglected, too, because you haven't sent her a note or anything, have you? You should call on her tomorrow.'

'I'll call on her now,' James said, rising to his feet and reaching for his walking sticks.

'No, no, it would be a waste of time and effort, she's confined to her bed-chamber today.

'Write her a note, by all means, so she knows she's not forgotten, and say you will call tomorrow. If she's not able to go downstairs tomorrow, she can write and tell you to avoid a wasted journey.'

James sat down again.

'Yes, that's a good idea.' He swept the papers on the desk to one side, and reached for a sheet of paper and his pen.

James didn't notice as Katherine pursed her lips, smiled to herself and swept from the room.

A short while later, James called for a footman.

'Take this note around to Lord Finch's house. You need not wait for a reply. Then go to Hatchard's bookshop in Piccadilly. You may tell him who you are and that you want a novel suitable for a lady of a tender disposition.

'It is for Lady Collins whom you know, should he enquire further, but do not name her. Tell him also that it is to be a handsome edition suitable as a gift. Is that clear?'

'Yes, my lord,' the footman replied and James waved him on his way.

Within the hour, the footman returned and placed a brown paper package tied with string upon the desk in front of James.

'The bookseller suggested this novel, my lord. If it does not suit I am to take it back immediately and he will find something else.'

James unwrapped the bundle to find it was a novel in three volumes and bound in fine leather with gilt lettering and gold edges to the paper. "Pride and Prejudice' by the author of 'Sense and Sensibility',' he read. He noticed the publication date of November 1813, so it was unlikely that Emma would have already read it.

'Thank you, that will be all.'

James turned a few pages carefully, so as to not crease the book, and started to read.

'It is a truth universally acknowledged, that a single man in possession of a good fortune must be in want of a wife.' Ah yes, how appropriate, he thought, I am certainly in want of a particular lady as my wife, I do hope she takes it as a hint, despite what she said the other day.

A Welcome Visit

The next morning, Emma was eager to get up and dressed. The doctor had said she might go downstairs, provided she had assistance and took care not to put too much weight on her twisted ankle. James had apologised in his letter for not knowing of her accident and said he would call on her this morning, so now she was in a hurry to get downstairs.

Molly helped her to the dressing table stool where she viewed her face in the mirror. She turned her head from side to side. The black and blue colouring was fading, only to be replaced by yellow shading.

'Perhaps some rice powder?' Molly ventured.

Emma sighed.

'No, I think I would need a vast quantity to hide it, and then it would keep falling off and making a mess. No, I don't think there is any point until it is mostly gone.'

Shortly, she was dressed in one of her smarter gowns and hobbling down the corridor, with an arm draped across Molly's shoulders. Getting down the stairs was a slow ordeal and Emma gained a better appreciation of how it must be for James.

Consequently she directed that they should continue down to the ground floor reception room, rather than stopping at the first floor morning-room. There she sat on the sofa, trembling slightly, and berating herself for behaving like a young nervous débutante.

After all, she was just waiting for a visit from a friend, wasn't she, even if the tone of his letter had been affectionate? Letters from friends were allowed to be affectionate, weren't they?

Emma hoped that James would come unfashionably early and she wouldn't have to sit there on her own all morning. She sent Molly off to order a tea tray to give herself something to do. She hadn't even finished her first cup when Lord Benfield was announced.

He paused in the doorway, his valet hovering behind him.

'Oh my dear, what have you done to yourself?' He hurried forward and sat next to her on the sofa, concern written on his face.

Norton quietly placed a package on the coffee table and raised an eyebrow at Molly before they both slipped quietly from the room.

'I foolishly slipped on the icy pavement,' Emma said almost tearfully, but feeling warm at being called his 'dear'.

James put his hand on her cheek and she leaned into it.

'Katherine says you twisted your ankle, sprained your wrist and I can see you have bruises. Are you in a lot of pain?'

'I'm feeling much better now, thank you,' Emma said, and she was. Having James there, who was clearly concerned for her and had his hand caressing her cheek, was definitely making her feel much better.

'Here, I have something for you,' James said, picking up the package and handing it to her. It was still wrapped in brown paper, but Katherine had found a length of red ribbon for James to make it make it a little more decorative.

Emma carefully unwrapped the books and felt the embossed cover with her hand.

'Oh,' she said, 'this is perfect. I have already read 'Sense and Sensibility' and it was wonderful, so I'm sure this will be, too. Ophelia gave me a Gothic novel to pass the time while I recuperate but it was awful and terribly depressing. This is so much better. Thank you.'

She leaned forward as if to kiss James when the door opened suddenly and Ophelia came into the room. Molly slipped in quietly behind her to sit in a chair in the corner behind the door.

'Emma!' Ophelia said. 'It is quite improper for you to be entertaining a gentleman with the door closed and no chaperone.'

'Ophelia, how can you suggest such a thing? My maid is sitting in the corner over there,' Emma said.

Ophelia whirled around in surprise, turned back to Emma and then took another confused look at Molly. Molly was obviously struggling to keep a straight face. Ophelia narrowed her eyes suspiciously and turned once more to Emma.

'Hmm, well, my apologies, I could have sworn she was out in the hallway.'

I'm sure she was in the hallway, Emma thought, carefully maintaining a virtuous expression, but some people don't notice servants until they're wanted.

'Now that I am up and about, perhaps we could choose a new date for the postponed dinner?' Emma asked, smiling innocently.

She suspected that Ophelia had hoped it would be forgotten, which was why Emma was now putting her on the spot. Ophelia couldn't very well refuse when Earl Benfield was sitting right in front of her.

'Yes, I suppose we should,' Ophelia said with no enthusiasm in her voice.

'Then what about tomorrow?' Emma asked. 'It was originally planned for yesterday, so the kitchen probably still have everything in readiness.'

Ophelia opened and closed her mouth like a fish, as she was losing control of the situation, much to Emma's satisfaction.

'It suits me, and I'm sure Victor and Katherine have nothing planned,' James said, following Emma's lead and boxing Ophelia further into the corner.

'Very well, I shall speak to chef,' a slightly bewildered Ophelia said, heading for the door. Molly sprang to her feet and quietly closed the door behind Ophelia, before Molly returned to her chair in the corner.

Emma and James grinned at each other. James glanced at Molly who was now looking intently at her fingernails. He reached for Emma's uninjured hand and rested it in his hand before caressing it gently.

He then picked it up and kissed the palm, watching one side of Emma's face blush pink while the other side remained resolutely blue and yellow.

'I must go,' he said. 'I have an errand

to run in the City, then I have to inform Victor and Katherine they are dining here tomorrow. I will see you then.'

James rose to his feet and Molly opened the door and beckoned James's valet to come in. Then she steadied Emma as she rose to her feet as well. Emma's hand remained closed as if to capture the kiss on her palm.

As James drove away, he tapped on the ceiling hatch with a walking stick.

'Yes, sir?' the groom said through the open hatch.

'To Rundell and Bridge on Ludgate Hill.' James hoped he could still remember the size of Emma's ring finger by the time they reached the jeweller's.

The One I Love

James and the Westons arrived for dinner in Stratton Street.

'Lord Weston,' Ophelia said, as they sipped pre-dinner drinks, 'I have told my husband that he and you are forbidden to talk politics this evening. I am well aware that you hold opposing views and I have no wish for blows to be exchanged at the dinner table. Besides which, the rest of us would probably be bored silly.'

'I'm sure we can agree to differ, Lady Finch, and reserve our shouting at each other for the House of Lords,' Victor said with a smile.

'Perhaps we should talk about children instead,' Lionel offered. 'My boys have given me little peace in the last few days. They are constantly talking about Astley's and the pantomime and wanting to know what we will do next.'

'So were my boys, until they heard that their cousins had been promised a pet dog, so now they keep dropping other hints,' Victor said.

The dessert finished, Ophelia rose from the table to be followed by Emma and Katherine.

'Finch, don't be too long over your port before joining us,' she said as she left the dining-room.

The butler placed decanters and glasses in front of the men as the footmen removed the remaining dishes from the table.

'Now then, gentlemen, you have tried the Portuguese claret,' Lionel said, 'so now try this port.

'I swear the quality of the wine improved as soon as we pushed Napoleon out of the country.'

The three of them savoured the bottle of port and agreed that it was definitely superior.

'As tempting as it is to stay here and finish this bottle,' Lionel said, 'I fear we must join the ladies promptly, as otherwise my wife will have my head.'

'Finch, I wonder if I might have a brief private word before we go through?' James asked.

'Victor, do go ahead, if you don't mind, and reassure them we are coming in a moment.'

Victor stood, nodded with a small smile on his lips and headed for the door. Once the door had clicked shut, James looked at Lionel.

'Finch, I know this is not strictly necessary, but I would like your permission, approval, whatever, to pay my addresses to Lady Collins,' James said.

'No, you are right, it's not at all necessary, but you have my wholehearted approval anyway.

'To be honest, when I've seen the two of you together, I've thought you already looked like a married couple and I'm sure you'll do well together.'

They grinned, shook hands, and Lionel stood up.

'Stay where you are and I'll send Emma in to see you.'

As Lionel left the dining-room for the drawing-room, James took some deep breaths.

He was about to offer marriage to

a lady, and while he had done it once before, it was a long time ago.

He thought and hoped Emma would accept him, especially after her throw-away remark of the other day, but there was no guarantee, and he felt very nervous.

He licked his lips which were suddenly dry.

As Lionel entered the drawing-room, several sets of eyes turned his way, expecting to see both him and James.

'Emma,' Lionel said, raising a finger to beckon her closer. He then spoke more quietly.

'Lord Benfield is still in the dining-room and would like a private word before he joins us, if you wouldn't mind.'

Emma's eyes widened slightly before she nodded and left the room, leaning on a walking stick as she went.

'James, you wanted to speak to me?'

'Yes, Emma dear, please come and sit with me a moment.'

Emma's heart lifted at the endearment.

He waited for her to sit next to him and then continued.

'Just recently I have been beset by nagging females.

'My daughters are constantly asking when they will see you next. Katherine is constantly telling me I should get married again.

'You are constantly telling me I should get out and about despite my difficulties. Frankly, it's all too much.'

Emma was dismayed. She had thought he was going to say something quite different. Her brows drew together and her mouth dropped open.

Her old doubts resurfaced, despite their meeting yesterday. Surely he wasn't going to tell her it was the last time they would meet?

'I can only tolerate one person nagging me,' James continued, 'and I have realised there is an obvious solution. I don't really mind you nagging me, because I love you, and if you would do me the honour of marrying me, the others will all hold their peace.'

Emma's eyes widened, her mouth snapped shut and a big smile spread across her face.

'Oh yes, please, I would like it above all things. I thought you were never going to ask. I've been comparing my other suitors to you, but they all fall far short because you're the one I love and no-one else would do.'

She leaned forward and cradled his face with her hands before kissing him squarely on the lips. James carefully cupped the back of her head with one hand while the other went around her back to pull her a little closer. After a few minutes they moved apart, but only slightly.

'Do you think the girls will mind?' Emma asked.

'Mind? They will be ecstatic. Call on me tomorrow if you can manage it and we shall tell them together. In the meantime, I have something for you.'

He reached into a pocket and drew out a small box, which he then opened and offered to her. It contained a ring with a sapphire centre and small diamonds surrounding it.

'Oh. Oh, James, it's lovely.' She blinked away the sudden dampness in her eyes before she took the ring from the box and put it on her finger.

'It fits perfectly.'

James smiled as he snapped the box closed and put it back in his pocket.

'We should go to the drawing-room and tell the others,' he said.

'Yes, certainly, but there's no hurry, is there?'

Several minutes later, they drew apart again.

'James, let us get married here in London and then go together to Baldock for Christmas.'

'That's very soon, although it would suit me perfectly. To do it we would need a special licence and also to talk to the vicar without delay.'

'I'm sure it can be arranged. Lionel is friends with the Bishop of Chertsey, so he could ask him. The House of Lords is closed for the season but I don't suppose

the bishop has gone far away.

'Then we could go together to your mother for Christmas. Afterwards the estimable Miss Williams can go with the girls to Oakham while we take a honeymoon trip to Spalding to tidy up my affairs.'

'I believe Spalding is very lovely at this time of year.'

Emma batted him on his arm.

'You've clearly been giving this some thought,' James said.

'I have been dreaming of little else for some time,' she replied with a broad smile.

'We really should join the others now. Ophelia might come bursting in, claiming that you have been compromised and insist we marry.'

Emma laughed as she pushed herself to her feet and took a firm grasp of her walking stick.

'My goodness, we do look a decrepit pair, don't we?' James said as he followed suit.

Happy News

The next morning Emma took the carriage around to Half Moon Street accompanied by a very cheerful Molly. They entered Weston House and Emma handed Molly her fur-lined pelisse and muff, taking in exchange a shawl more suited for indoor wear.

'Molly,' Emma said, with a twinkle in her eye, 'since I am now betrothed, I don't need you to act as my chaperone and I'm steady on my feet today as well.

'Why don't you go down to the serv-ants' hall for a cup of tea and a chat with whoever might be there? If you can find Norton, he could introduce you to the others. After all, you do now need to get to know the people here.'

'Thank you, my lady,' Molly said, grinning as she passed the clothing to a footman to put in the hall cupboard.

The butler conducted Emma to the morning-room where she found James sitting on a sofa with his daughters.

'Good morning, James. Good morning, Sarah. Good morning, Helen,' she said.

'Good morning, Lady Collins,' the girls chorused.

'Good morning, Emma,' James said. 'Come and sit with us on the sofa.

'Lady Collins,' Sarah said, looking concerned, 'Papa told us how you slipped on some ice and hurt yourself. Is it very painful?'

'Thank you, Sarah, I am much better already and my bruises are starting to fade,' Emma said, indicating her face.

Sarah scooted sideways to make room, so that she and her sister were between James and Emma.

'Now, girls, you remember I said I had something to tell you when Lady Collins arrived?'

They nodded, full of curiosity and looking from their father to Emma and back.

'Yesterday I asked Lady Collins to marry me and she agreed. She is going to be your new mama.

'What do you think of that?'

'Oh, Papa,' Sarah said, her eyes round with surprise, 'that is wonderful.' She turned to Emma.

'Will you be coming to live with us? Every day? And go home with us to Oakham?'

'I should like that very much,' Emma said. 'I have always wished I had two daughters just like you two.'

'Will you tell us bedtime stories, too?' Helen asked.

'I will love to be telling you bedtime stories. I only hope I can think of enough of them.'

She kissed them both on the forehead before fondly looking across to James.

'We need to find Christmas presents for your cousins,' James said, 'so I thought we could all go together to Mr Hamley's Ark and see if we can find something suitable.'

'Yes, Papa, but you don't need to get anything for us,' Sarah said, taking Emma's arm and leaning her head against it. 'You have just given us the best gift for Christmas ever!'

Emma looked at James with glistening eyes and a frog in her throat. She cleared her throat and swallowed.

'We are going to get married in the next day or two. Now, when a lady gets married, it's usual for her to have a couple of bridesmaids to attend her. I wondered if you two girls would be the bridesmaids for me?'

The girls' eyes went big and round.

'What would we have to do?' Sarah whispered, awestruck.

'Well . . . You would wear your best dresses and follow me into the church. You would make sure my dress didn't get tangled on anything and when I get to the front where your papa will be standing, you can look after my flowers for me.'

'Where can we get flowers at this time of year?' James asked, while the girls were thinking this through.

'I'll ask Katherine to get her modiste to make a bouquet in two parts from silk flowers.'

'I can see I will be glad to have a wife

who is a competent organiser,' James said, who was rewarded with a happy smile from his fiancée.

'Lady Collins,' a thoughtful Helen piped up, 'can we call you Mama?'

'Helen,' Emma said, 'I shall be very, very happy to have two lovely daughters who call me Mama.'

Tears of Joy

Three days later, Emma's carriage drew up at the steps of St George's Church, Hanover Square. At the top of the steps was Miss Williams, who was holding hands with Sarah and Helen. The girls were wearing the same white dresses as they had worn when Emma met them at the inn in Sawtry.

The dresses were not especially fancy for the occasion, but Emma had thought them appropriate. If she had not started talking to them at the inn, everything else may never have happened.

Anyway, in practical terms, there was no time to get anything more opulent made.

Emma was wearing a dark green dress that had been an evening dress until two days ago, before rapid adjustments were undertaken by Molly.

Everybody was wearing a warm cloak, as a chill wind was whistling past the columns at the front of the church.

Once they were all inside the doors, they threw back their cloaks over their shoulders, rather than remove them. The church was not much warmer than the weather outside. Emma looked down the aisle and could see James and Victor, who were both looking towards her. Right at the far end she could see the rector, the Reverend Hodgson. Ophelia had not dared suggest the Reverend Goodman marry them.

To either side near the altar, was a hastily recruited small choir dressed in white surplices, then the first few rows of pews were filled with family members and all the staff who could be spared.

'Ready?' Lionel asked.

Emma looked back at the two girls, who looked a little nervous. She smiled reassuringly at them before turning back to her brother.

'Ready,' she said, and they started up the aisle.

When they reached a broadly smiling James, she released Lionel's arm and turned to the girls, giving them each half of her bouquet.

Lionel guided them to the first pew where a space had been left next to their grandmother, who was dabbing at her eyes with a lacy handkerchief.

'Grandmama, don't be sad,' Sarah whispered.

'Oh, I'm not sad,' she whispered back, 'I'm just so very, very happy.'

Once the vows had been said and the register signed, Emma and James made their slow way back down the aisle. James was holding Emma's elbow, rather than the other way around, and was holding a single walking stick in his other hand.

'I hope you don't mind supporting me like this,' he said, quietly, to his new countess.

'Of course not, now we can support each other. After all that is what marriage is about, isn't it?'

We do hope that you have enjoyed reading this large print book.

Did you know that all of our titles are available for purchase?

We publish a wide range of high quality large print books including:
Romances, Mysteries, Classics
General Fiction
Non Fiction and Westerns

Special interest titles available in large print are:
The Little Oxford Dictionary
Music Book, Song Book
Hymn Book, Service Book

Also available from us courtesy of Oxford University Press:
Young Readers' Dictionary
(large print edition)
Young Readers' Thesaurus
(large print edition)

For further information or a free brochure, please contact us at:
Ulverscroft Large Print Books Ltd.,
The Green, Bradgate Road, Anstey,
Leicester, LE7 7FU, England.
Tel: (00 44) **0116 236 4325**
Fax: (00 44) **0116 234 0205**

BLETCHLEY SECRETS

Dawn Knox

1940: A cold upbringing with parents who unfairly blame her for a family tragedy has robbed Jess of all self-worth and confidence. Escaping to join the WAAF, she's stationed at RAF Holsmere, until a seemingly unimportant competition leads to her recruitment into the secret world of code-breaking at Bletchley Park. Love, however, eludes her: the men she chooses are totally unsuitable — until she meets Daniel. But there is so much which separates them. Can they ever find happiness together?

THE LOMBARDI EMERALDS

Margaret Mounsdon

Who is Auguste Lombardi, and why has May's mother been invited to his eightieth birthday party? As her mother is halfway to Australia, and May is resting between acting roles, she attends in her place. To celebrate the occasion, she wears the earrings her mother gave her for her birthday — only to discover that they are not costume jewellery, but genuine emeralds, and part of the famous missing Lombardi collection . . .

TURPIN'S APPRENTICE

Sarah Swatridge

England, 1761. Charity Bell is the daughter of an inn keeper. Her two elder sisters are only interested in marrying well, whereas feisty Charity is determined to discover who the culprit is behind the most recent highwayman ambush. And by catching the highwayman, she aims to persuade Sir John to bring his family, and his wealth, to her village. It may also make the handsome Moses notice her!

REVENGE OF THE SPANISH PRINCESS

Linda Tyler

Cornwall, 1695. When her beloved father dies with the name Lovett on his lips, privateer captain Catherina Trelawny vows revenge on the mysterious pirate. Seeking him on the Mediterranean island of Azul, she is charmed by the personable Henry Darley. But Cate finds her plan goes awry when Darley and Lovett turn out to be the same man. Cate and Henry set sail across the high seas battling terrifying storms, deadly shipwreck, dissolute corsairs — and each other.